SHaPeS

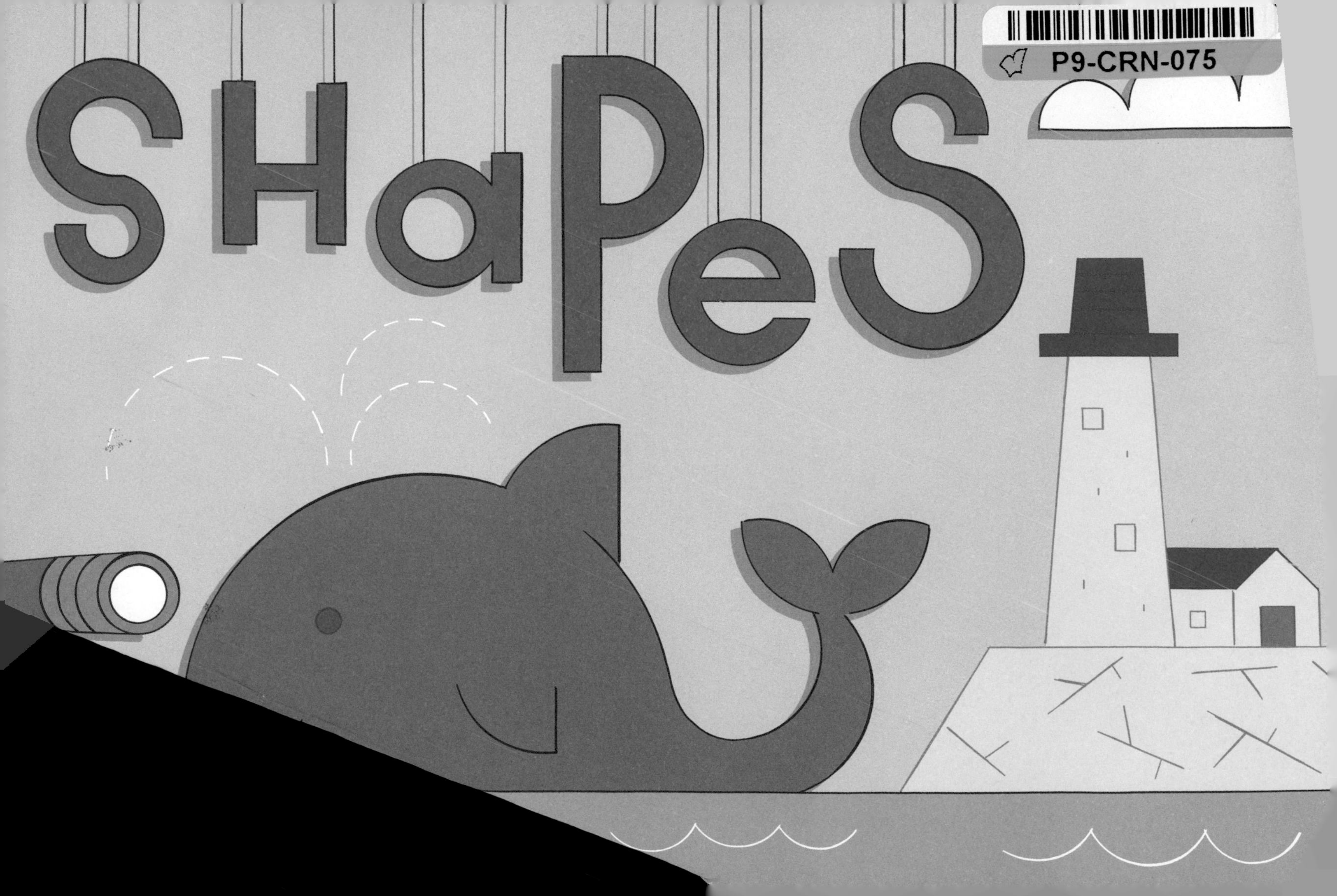

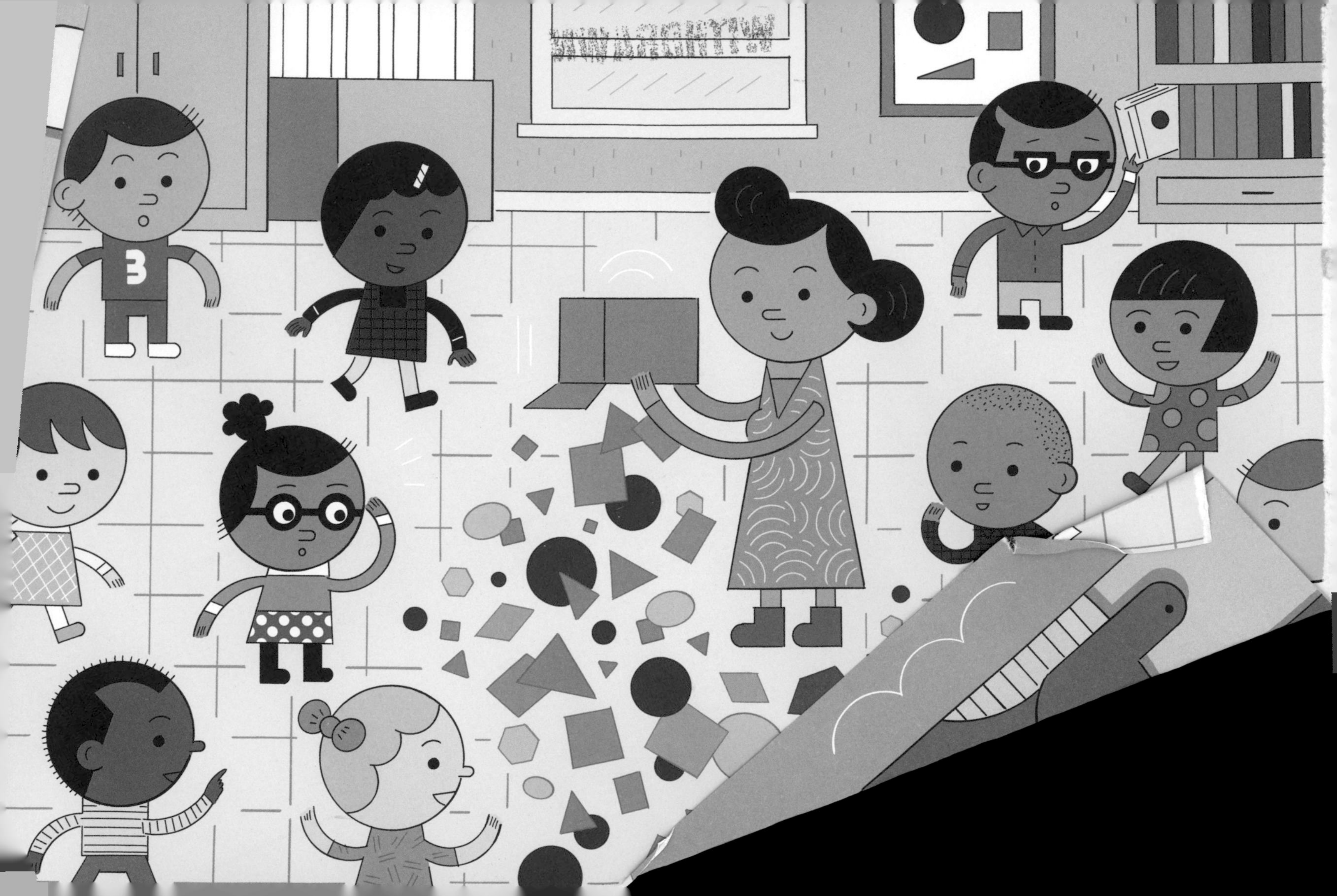

ShAPEs aNd SHaPeS

WITH ANNEMARIE

A TOON BOOK BY

ivan brunetti

For Laura

Editorial Director: FRANÇOISE MOULY

Book Design: IVAN BRUNETTI & FRANÇOISE MOULY

IVAN BRUNETTI'S artwork was done in India ink and colored digitally.

A TOON Book™ © 2023 Ivan Brunetti & TOON Books, an imprint of Astra Books for Young Readers, a division of Astra Publishing House. Copying or digitizing this book for storage, display, or distribution in any other medium is strictly prohibited. All rights reserved. For information about permission to reproduce selections from this book, please contact permissions@astrapublishinghouse.com. TOON Books®, TOON Graphics™, and TOON Into Reading!™ are trademarks of Astra Publishing House. Library of Congress Cataloging-in-Publication Data: Names: Brunetti, Ivan, author, illustrator. Title: Shapes and shapes : Toon Level 1 / Ivan Brunetti. Description: New York : TOON Books, an imprint of Astra Books for Young Readers, a division of Astra Publishing House, [2023] | "A Toon book"--Title page. | Audience: Grades K-1 | Summary: "In this fun, educational STEAM graphic novel by a master cartoonist, a diverse group of elementary school students learn about geometry and the simple shapes that make up our world, in both the classroom and the playground"--Provided by publisher. | Identifiers: LCCN 2022060781 | ISBN 9781662665172 (hardcover) | ISBN 9781662665189 (paperback) | ISBN 9781662665196 (ebk) Subjects: LCSH: Shapes--Juvenile literature. | Shapes--Comic books, strips, etc. Classification: LCC QA445.5 .B784 2023 | DDC 516/.15--dc23/eng20230302 LC record available at https://lccn.loc.gov/2022060781 All our books are Smyth Sewn (the highest library-quality binding available) and printed with soy-based inks on acid-free, woodfree paper harvested from responsible sources. Printed in China. First edition.

ISBN: 978-1-6626-6517-2 (hardcover)   ISBN: 978-1-6626-6518-9 (paperback)

10 9 8 7 6 5 4 3 2 1

WWW.TOON-BOOKS.COM

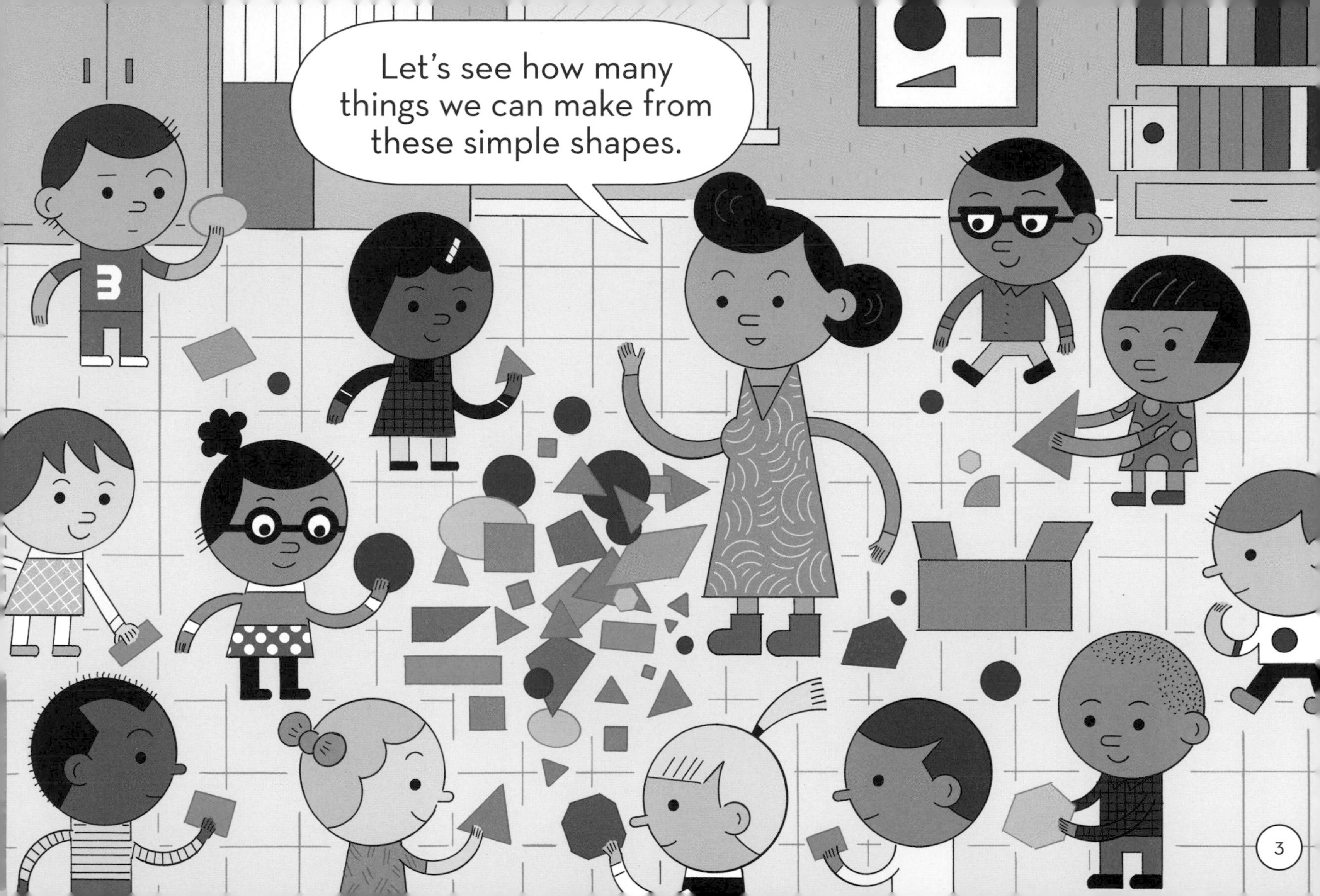
Let's see how many things we can make from these simple shapes.

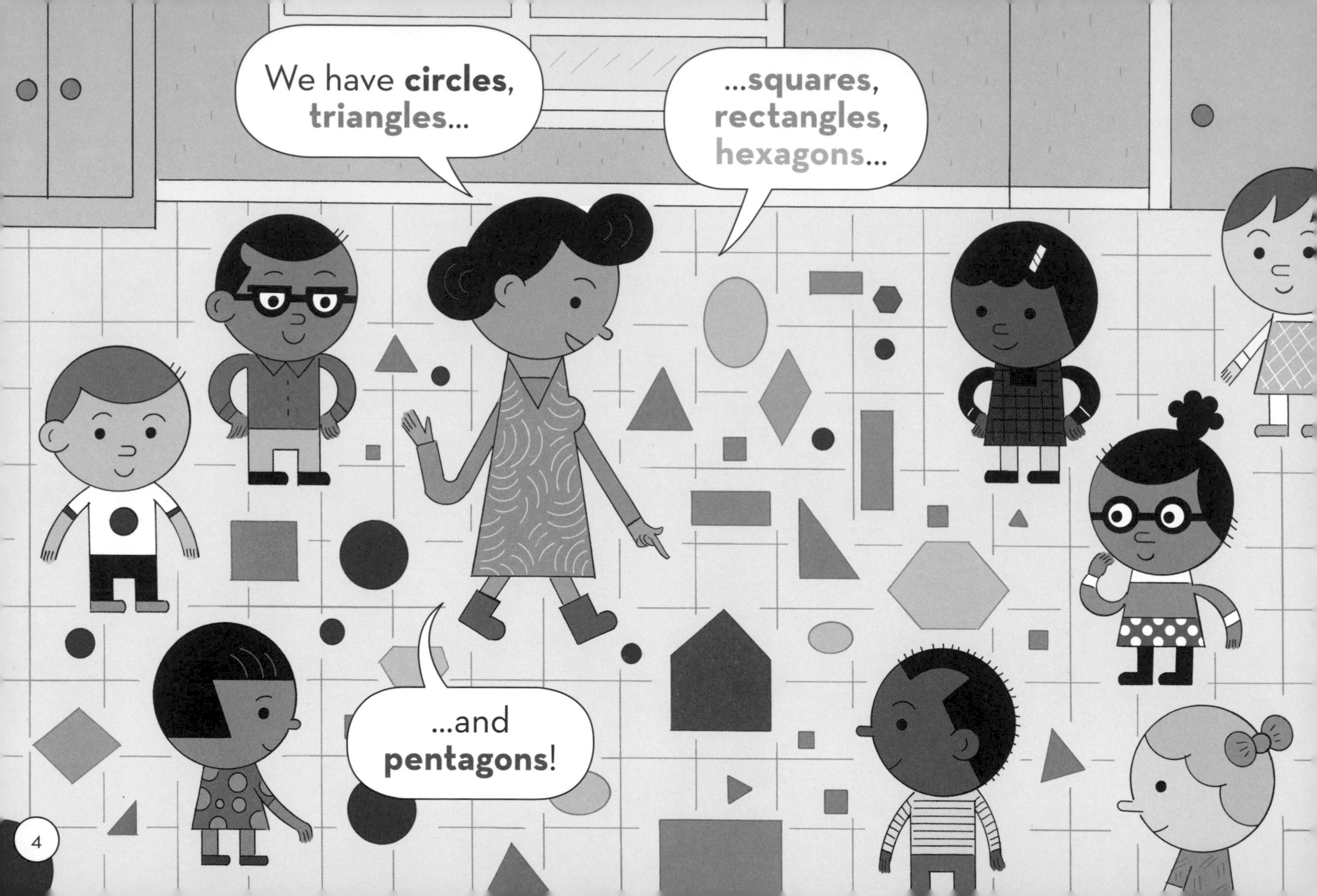
We have **circles**, **triangles**...
...**squares**, **rectangles**, **hexagons**...
...and **pentagons**!

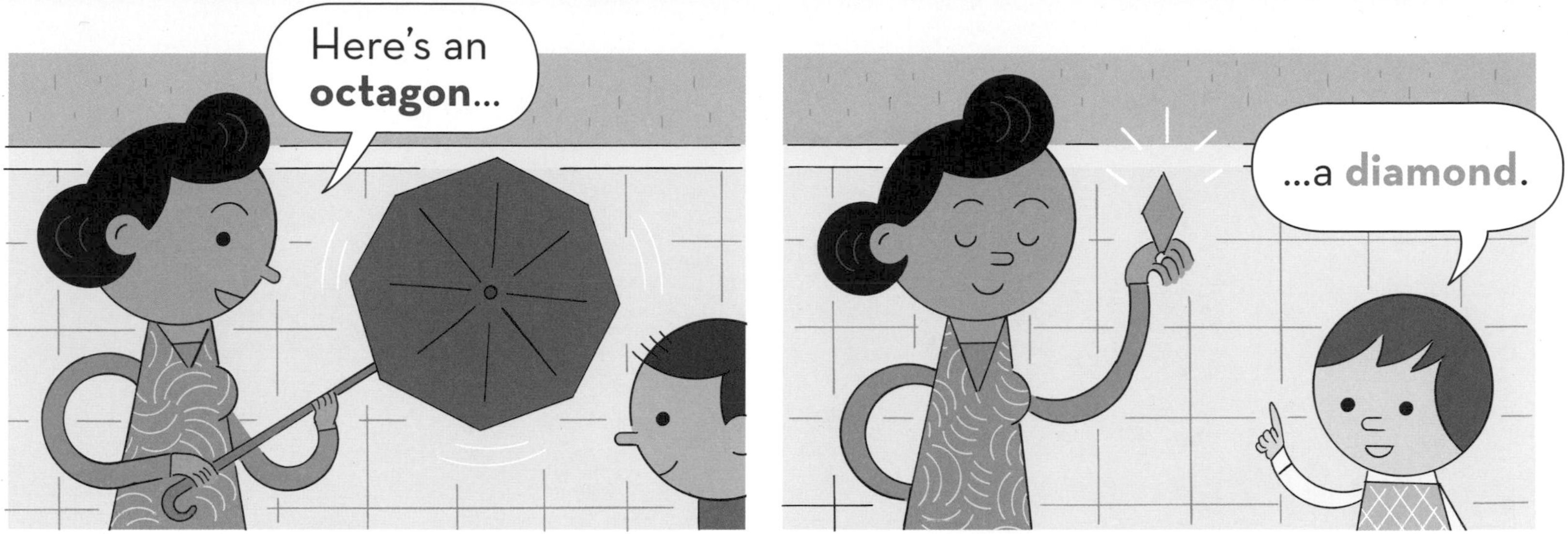
Here's an **octagon**...
...a **diamond**.

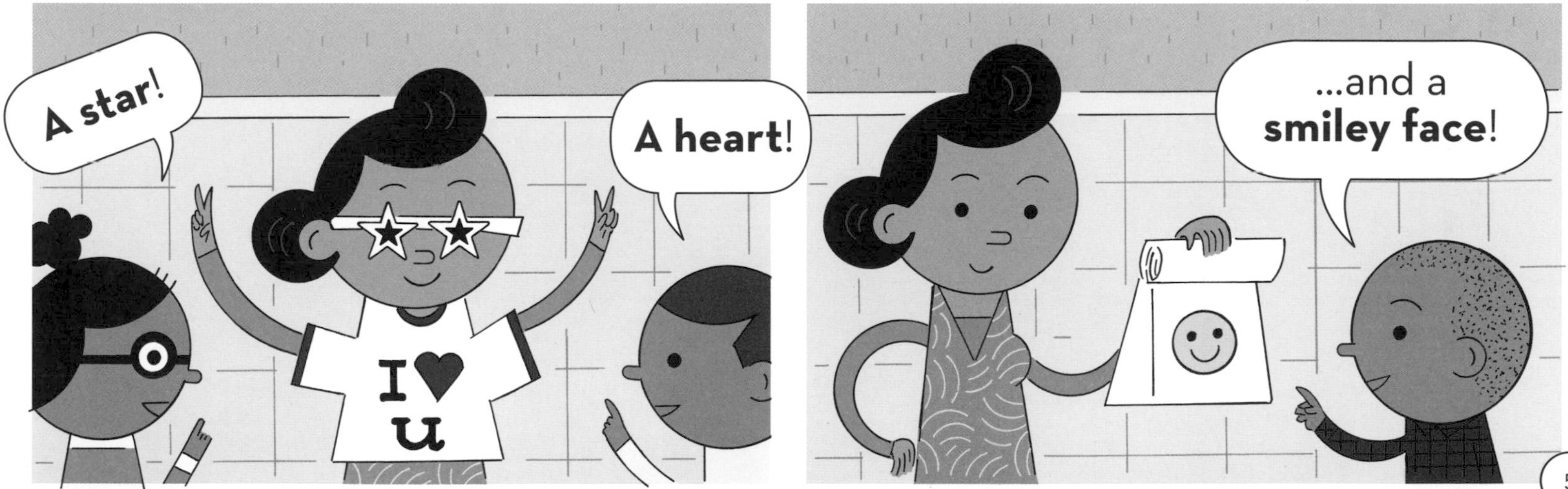
A star!
A heart!
I ♥ u
...and a **smiley face**!

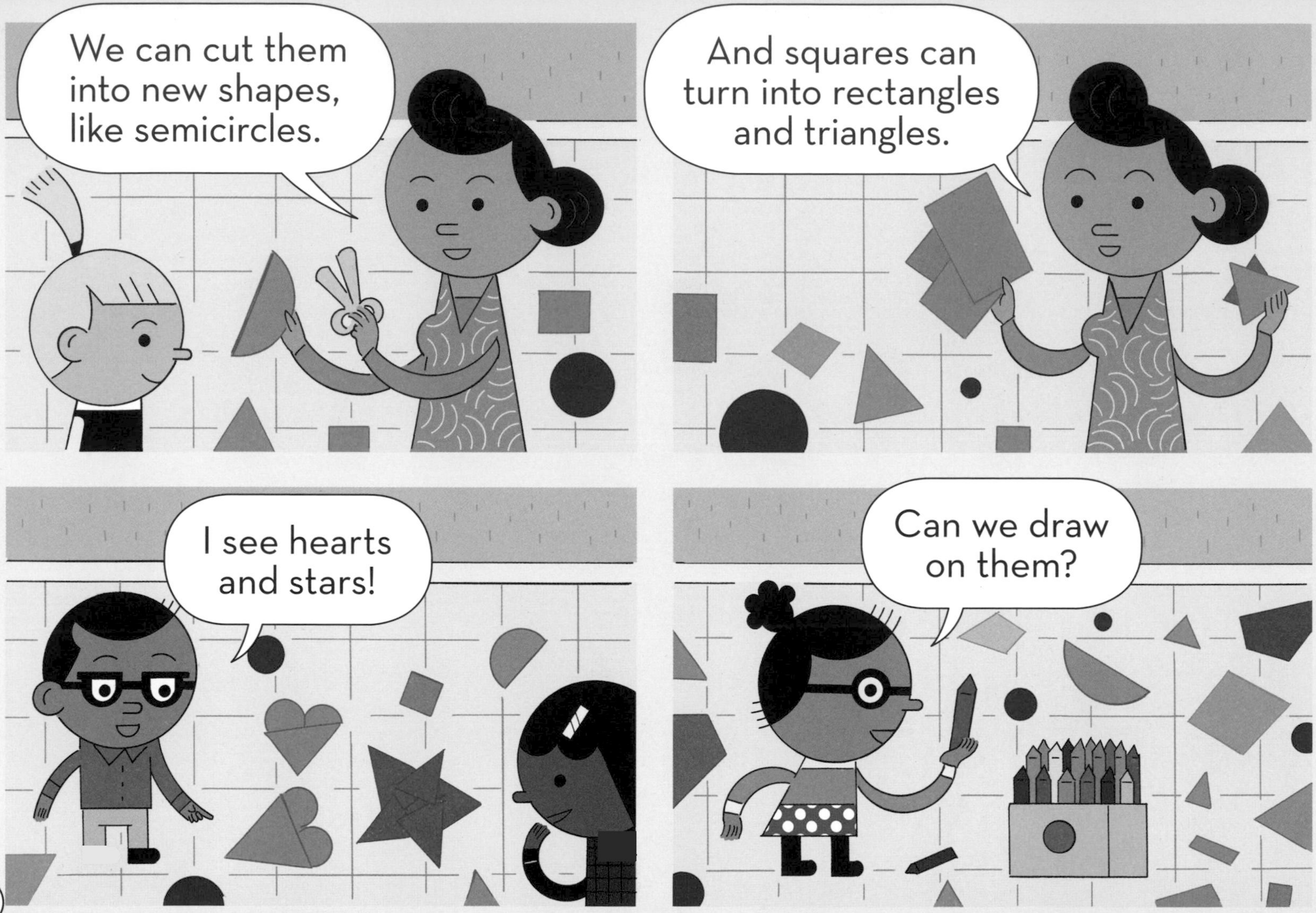
We can cut them into new shapes, like semicircles.
And squares can turn into rectangles and triangles.
I see hearts and stars!
Can we draw on them?

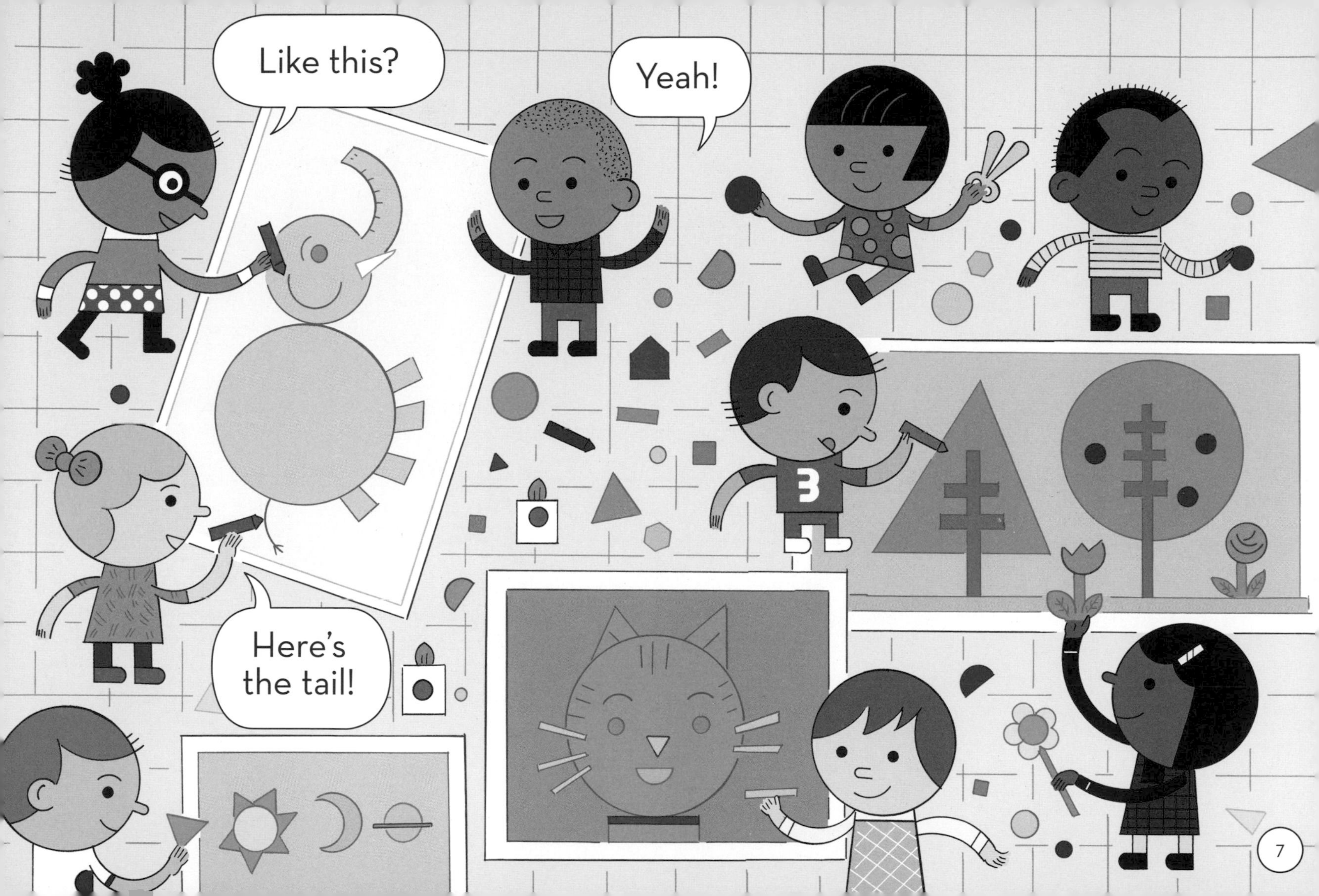
Like this?
Yeah!
Here's the tail!

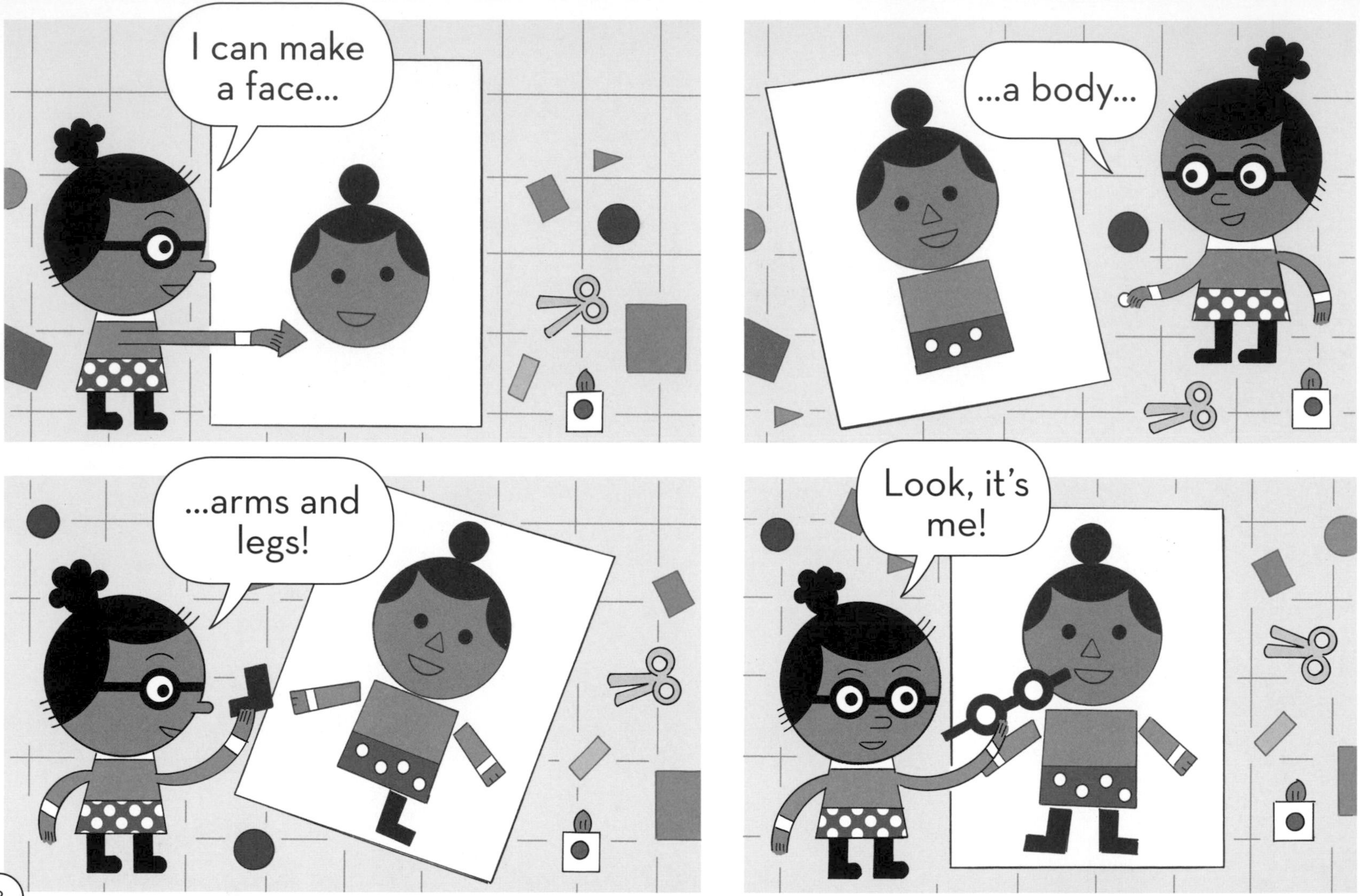
I can make a face...
...a body...
...arms and legs!
Look, it's me!

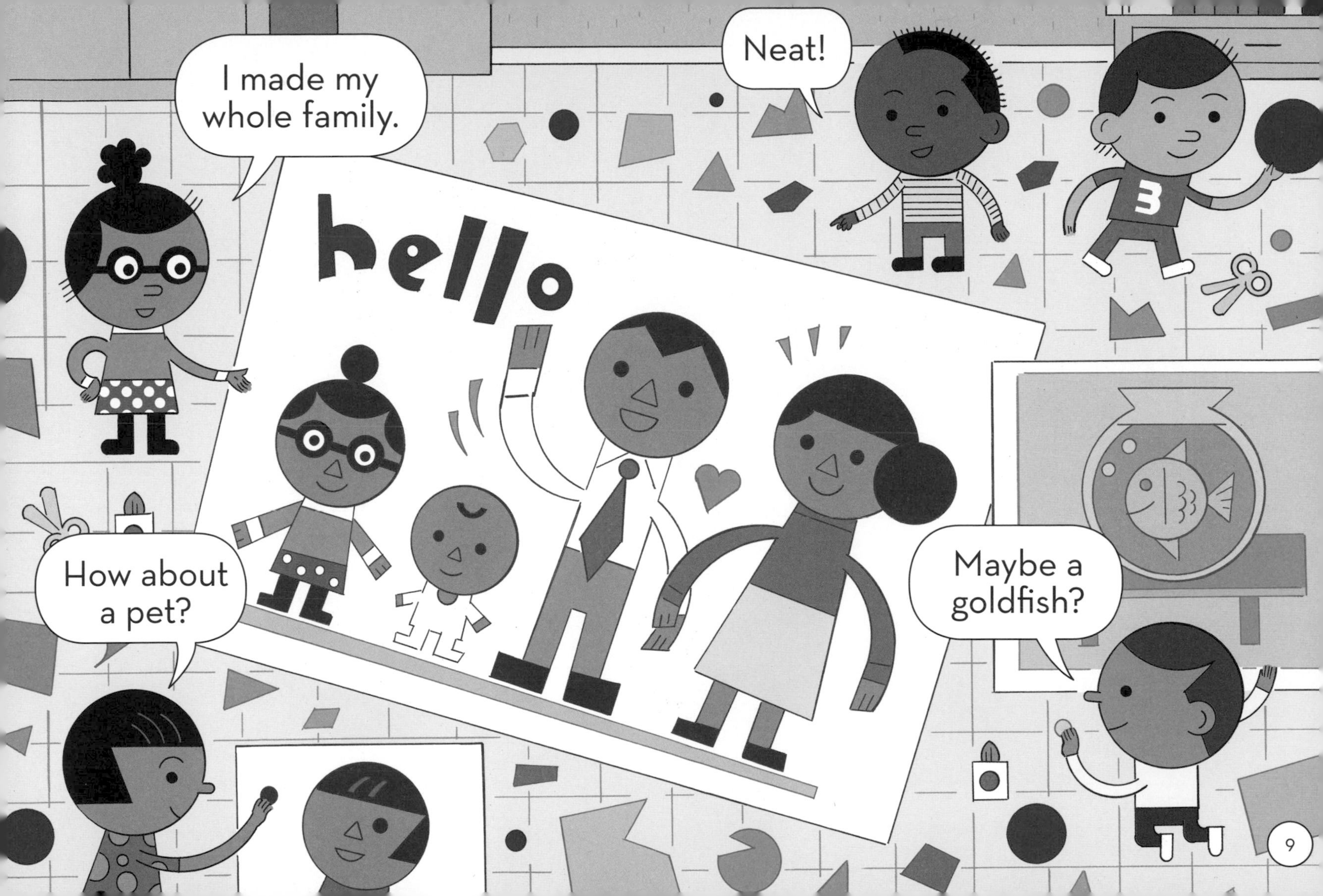
I made my whole family.
Neat!
hello
How about a pet?
Maybe a goldfish?

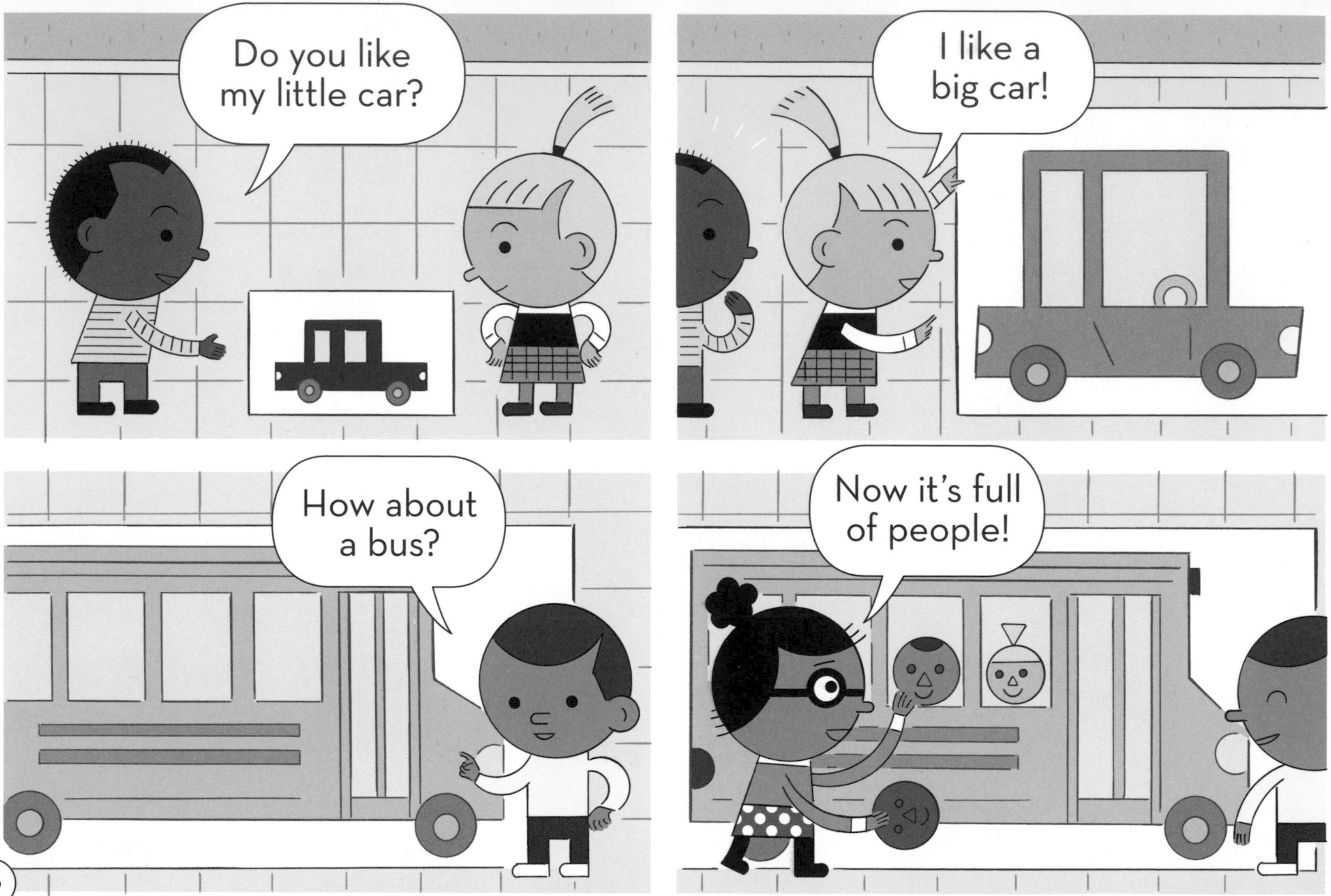
Do you like my little car?
I like a big car!
How about a bus?
Now it's full of people!

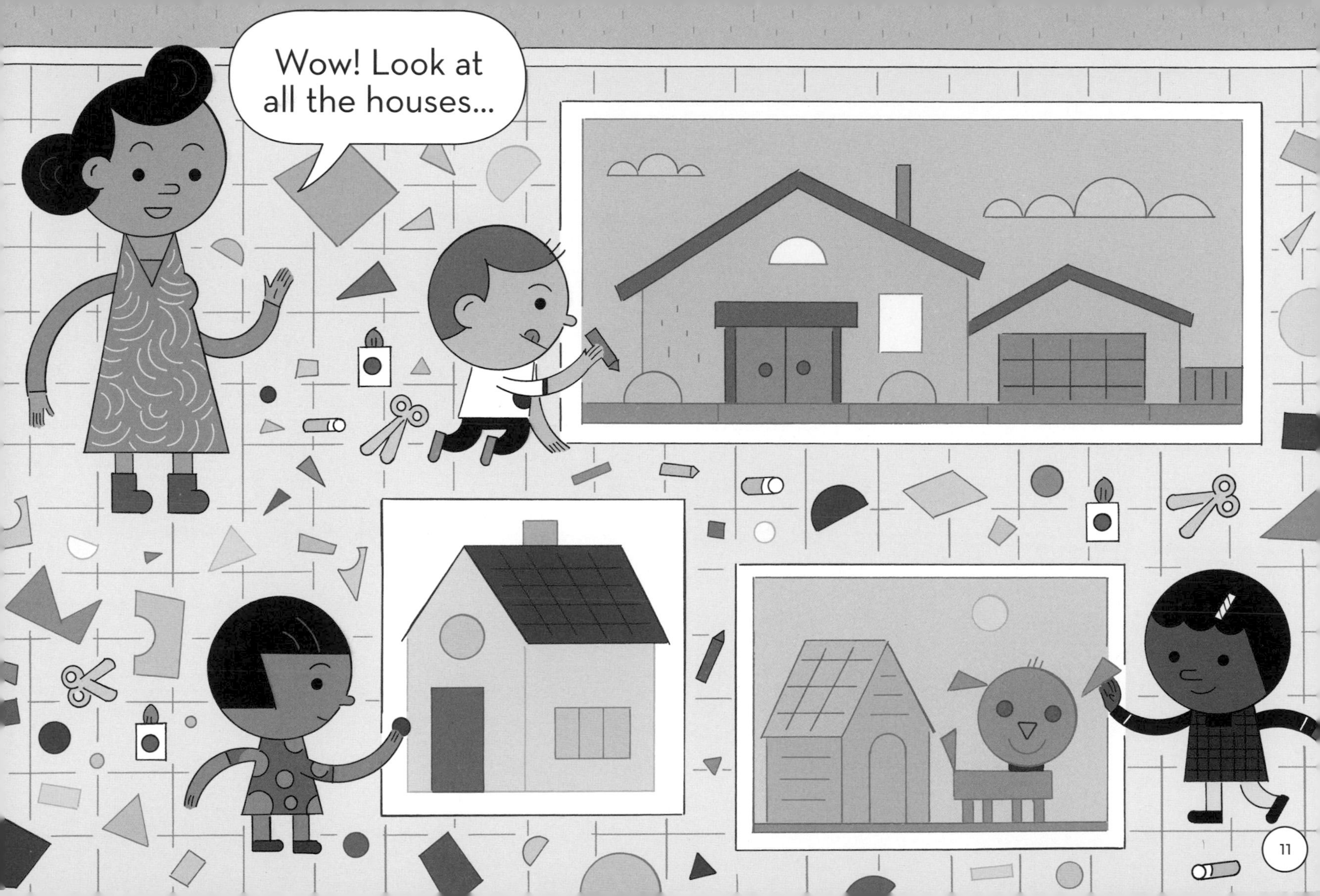
Wow! Look at
all the houses...

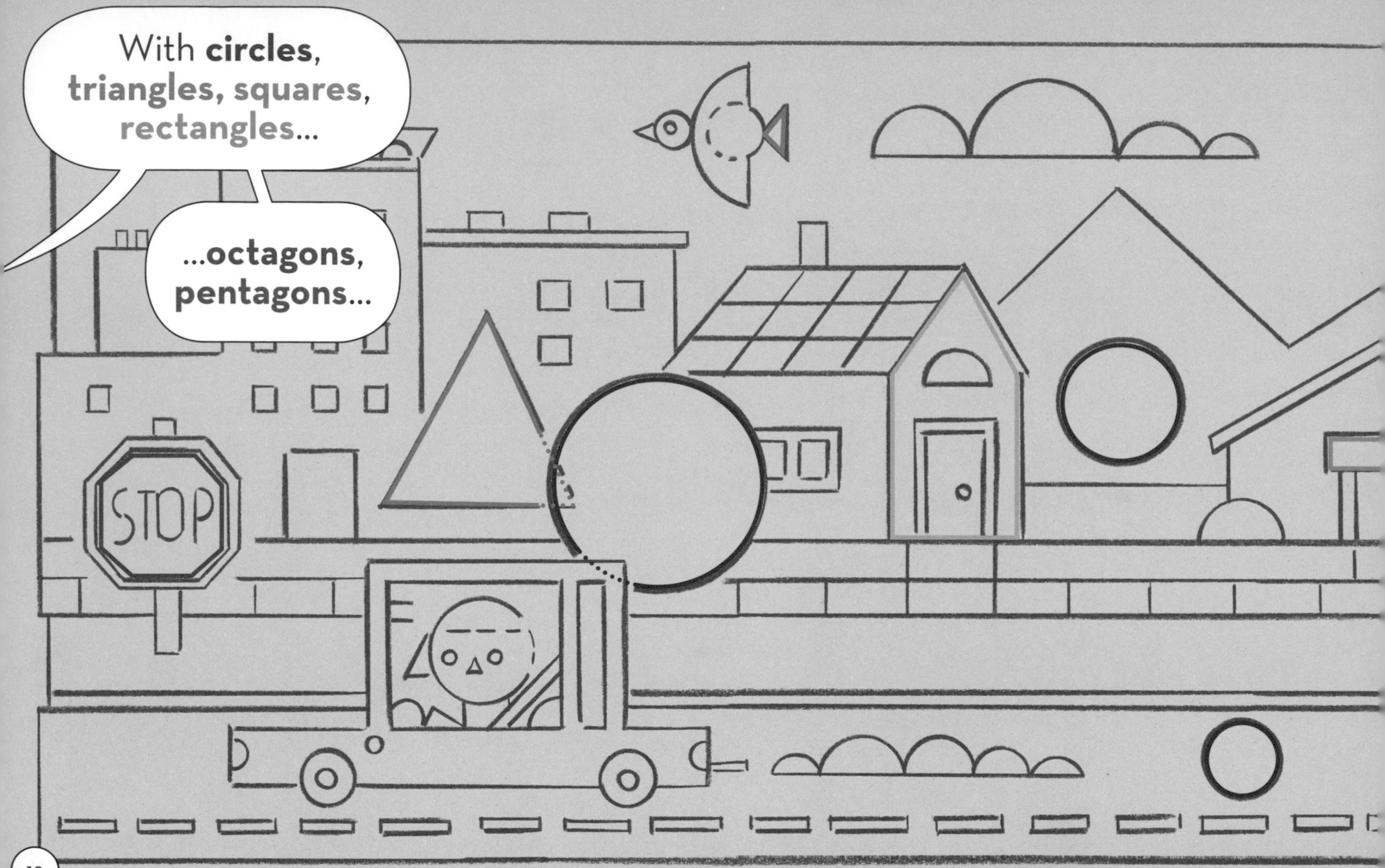
With **circles**, **triangles, squares, rectangles**...
...**octagons, pentagons**...
STOP

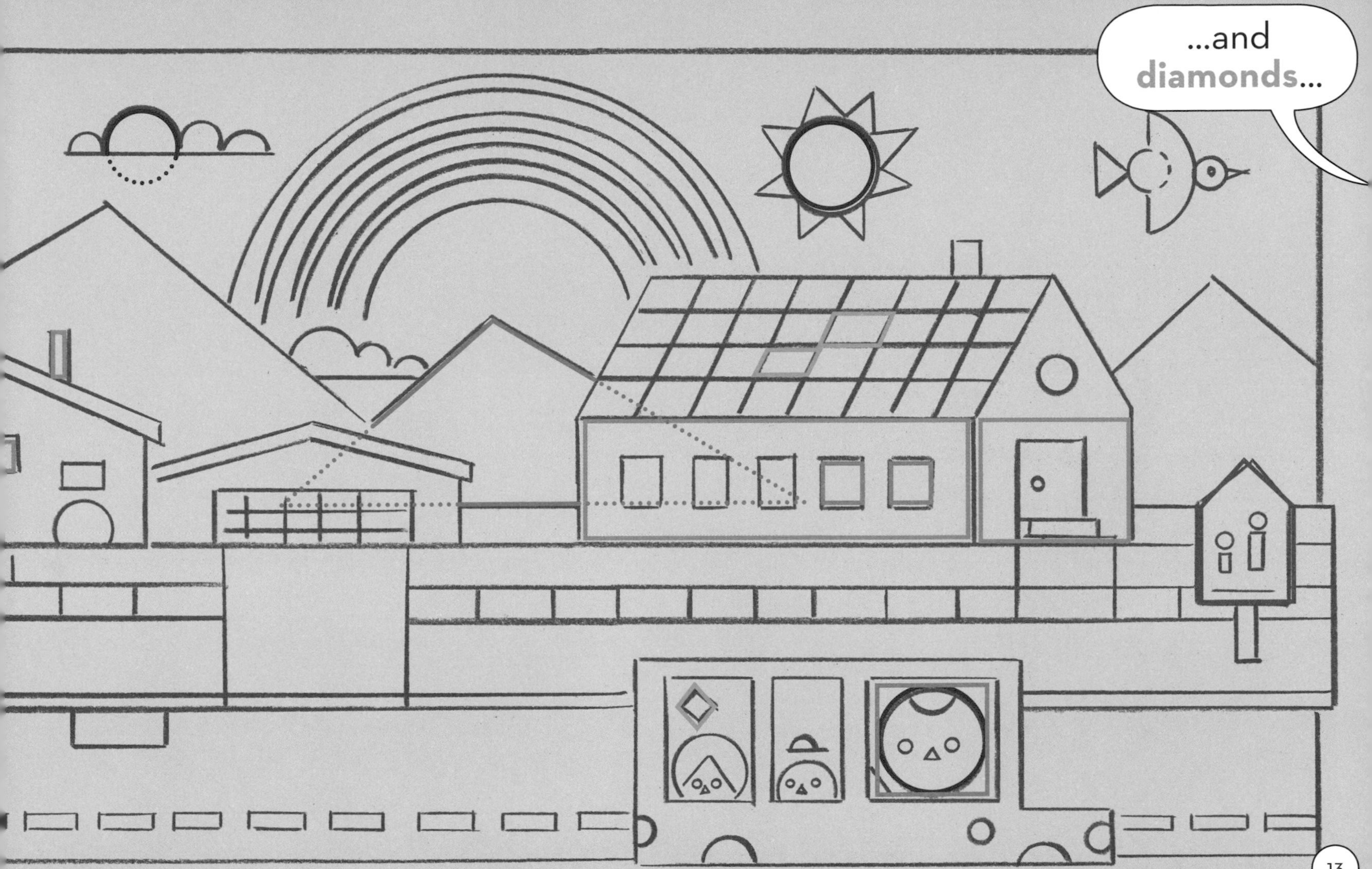
...and
diamonds...

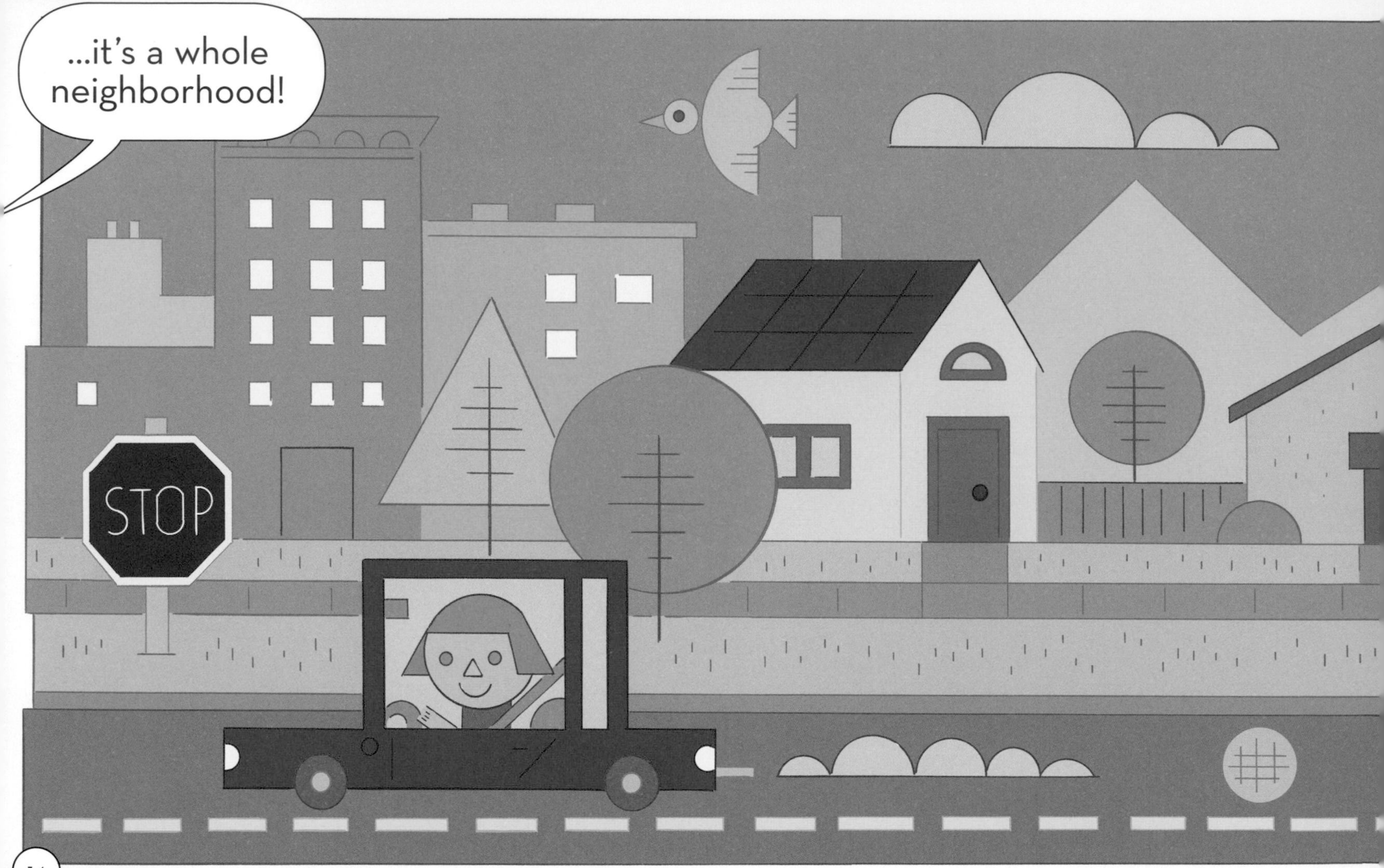
...it's a whole neighborhood!
STOP

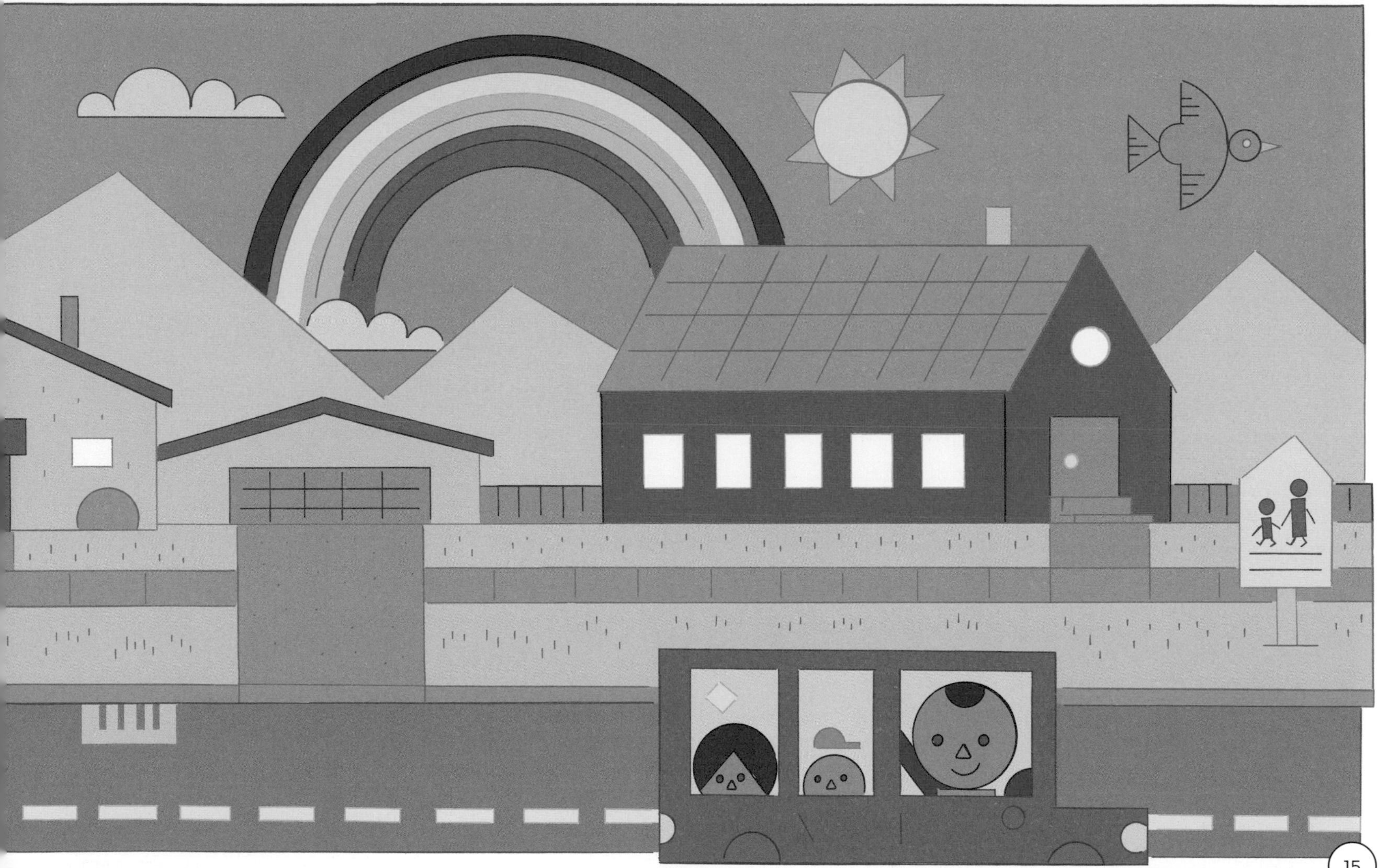

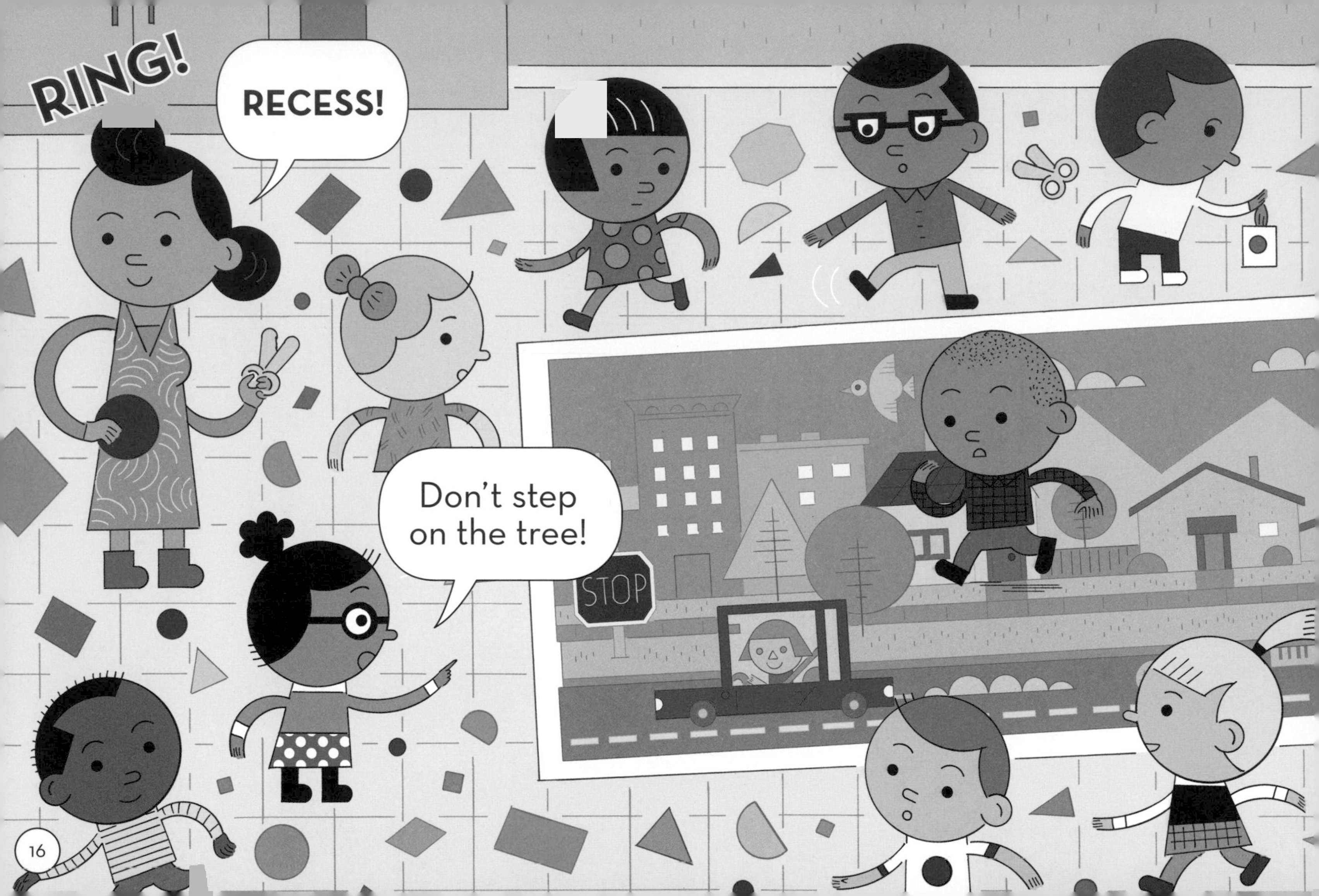
RING!
RECESS!
Don’t step on the tree!
STOP

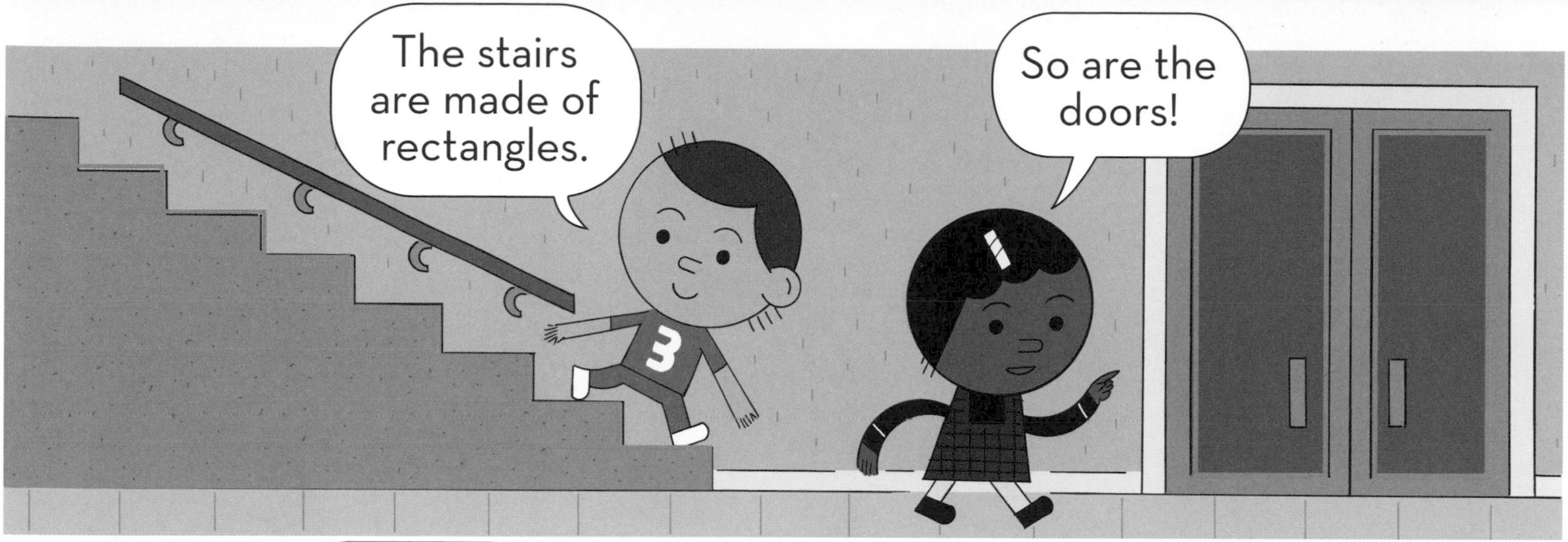
The stairs are made of rectangles.
So are the doors!

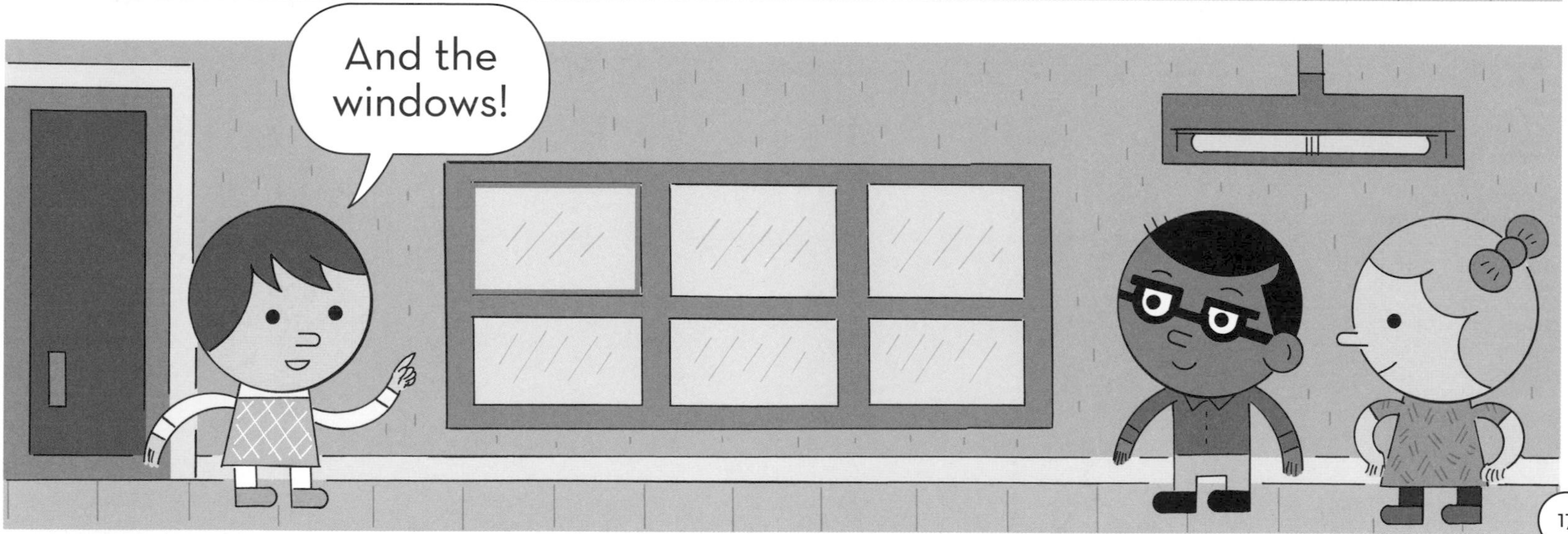
And the windows!

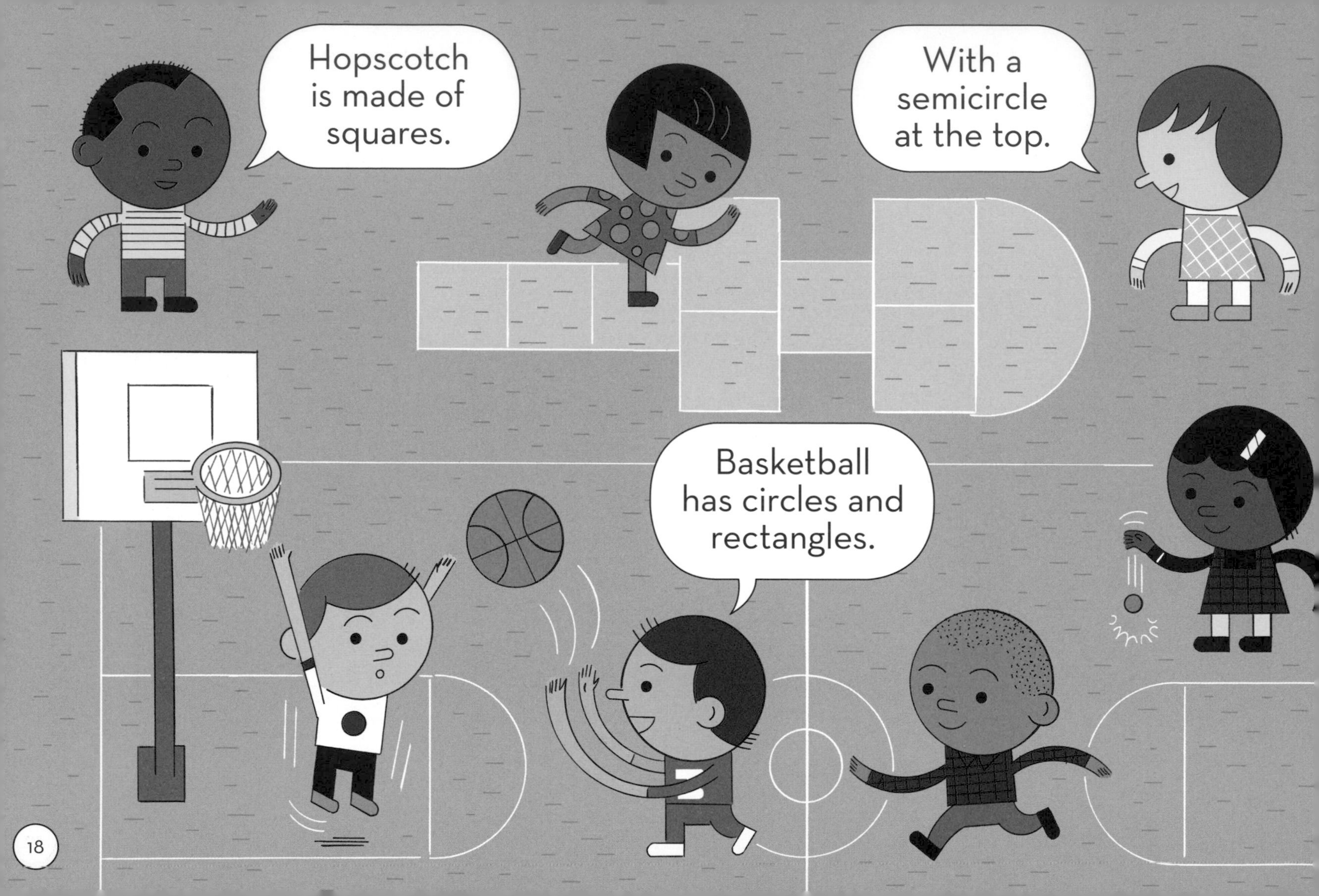
Hopscotch is made of squares.
With a semicircle at the top.
Basketball has circles and rectangles.

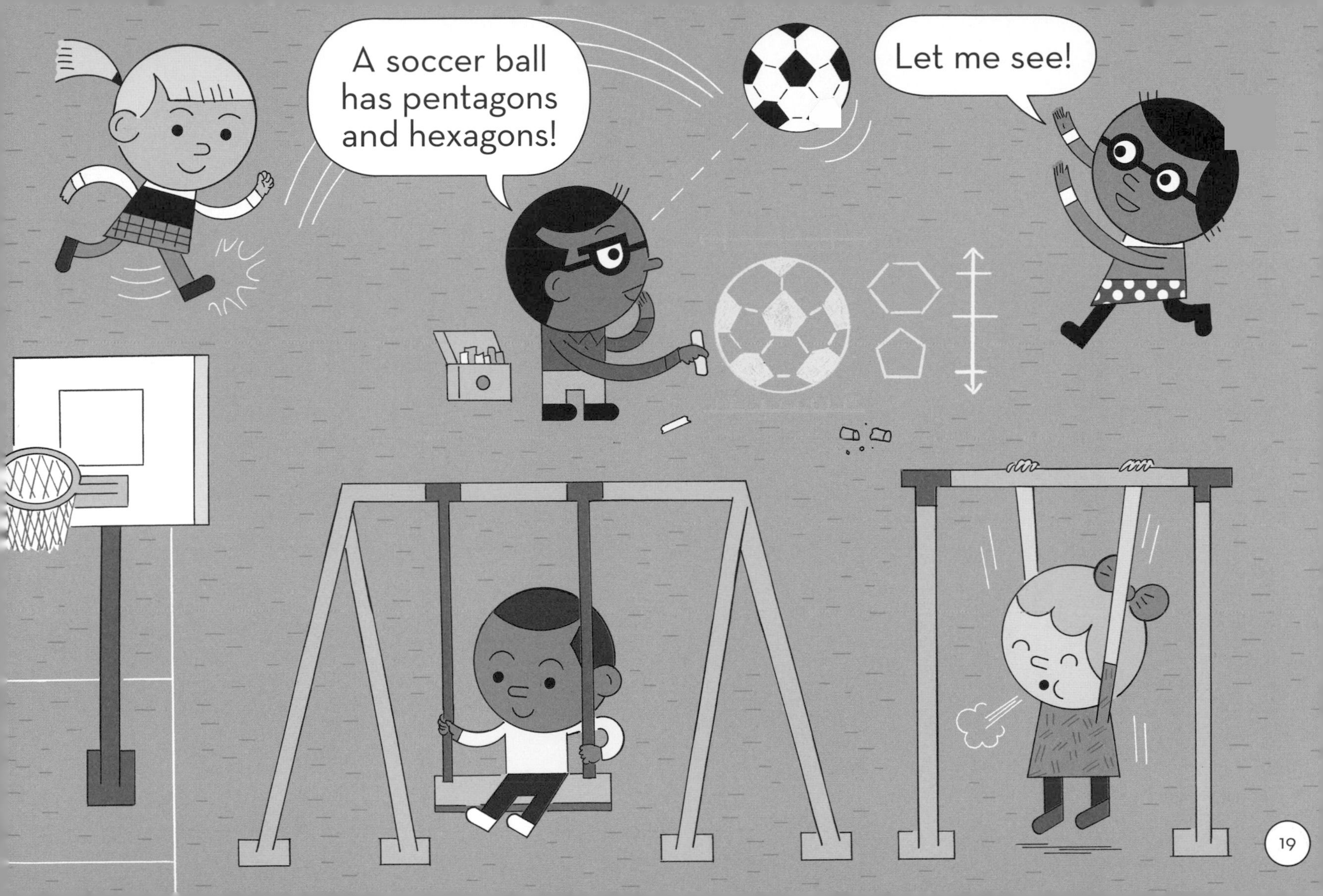
A soccer ball has pentagons and hexagons!
Let me see!

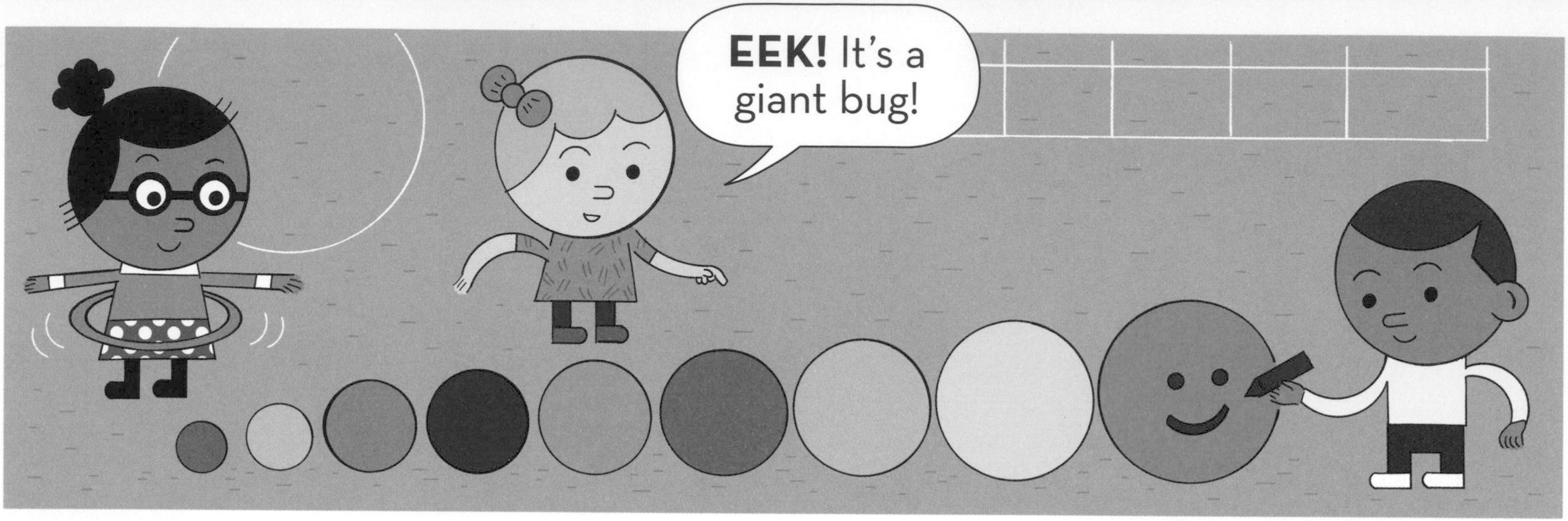
EEK! It's a giant bug!

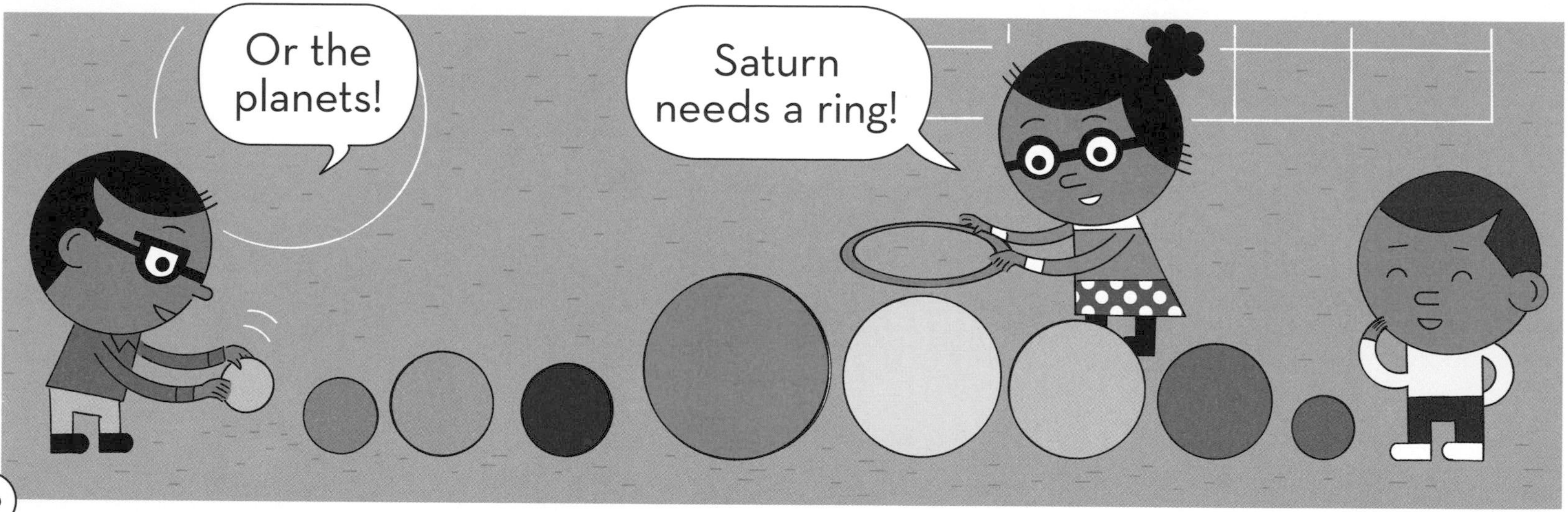
Or the planets!
Saturn needs a ring!

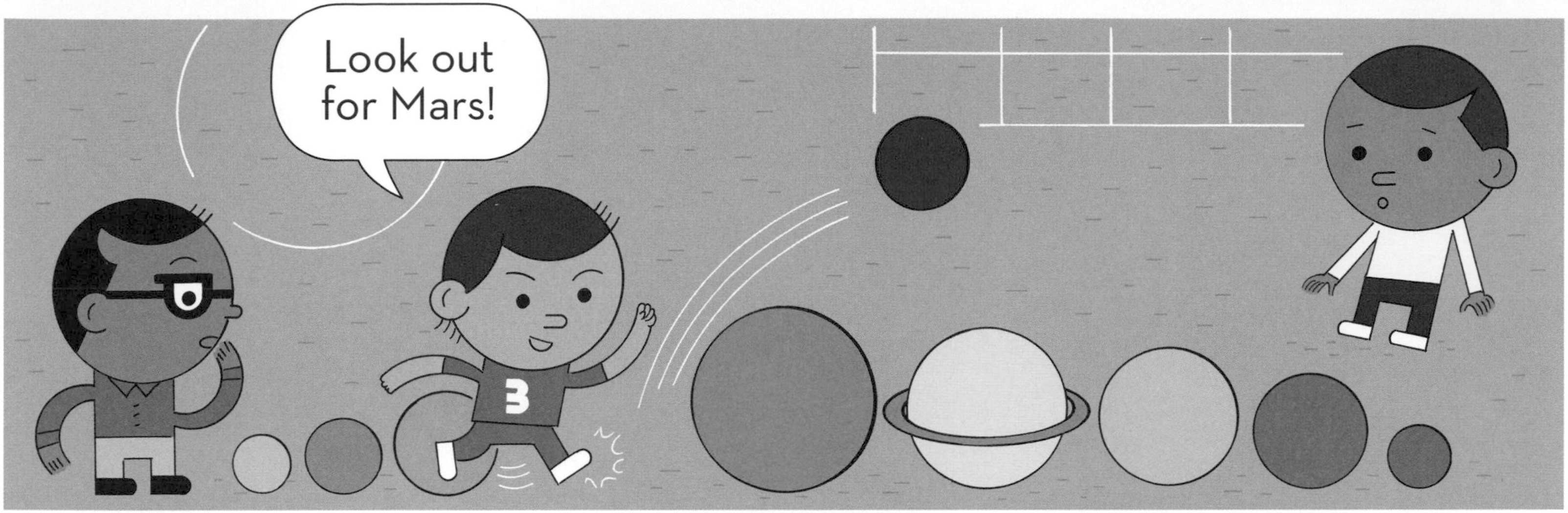
Look out
for Mars!

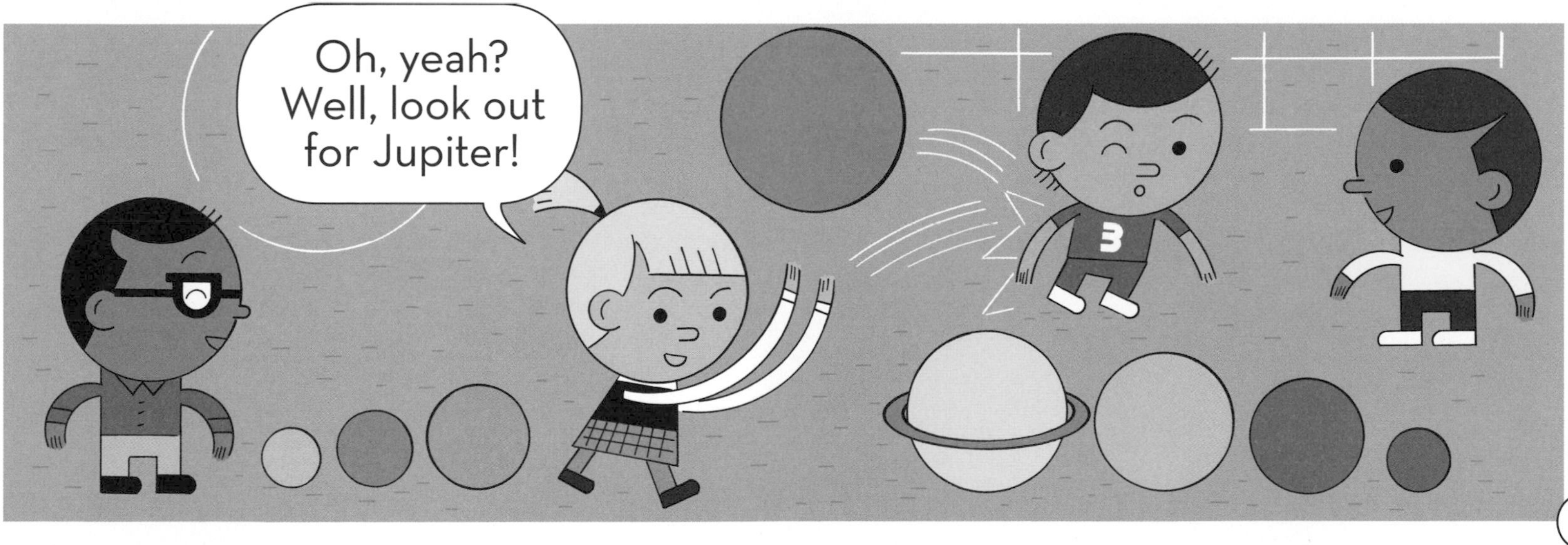
Oh, yeah?
Well, look out
for Jupiter!

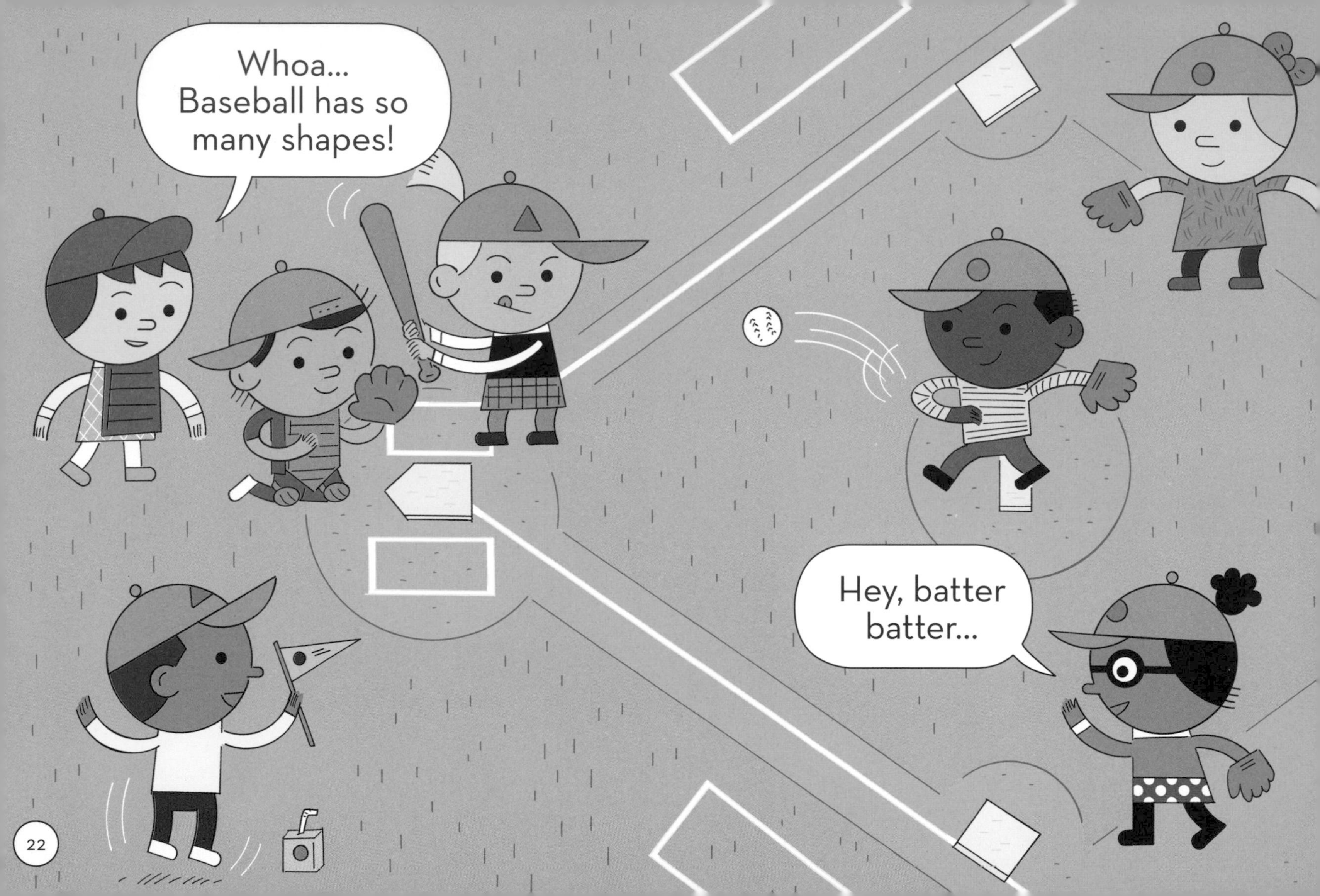
Whoa... Baseball has so many shapes!
Hey, batter batter...

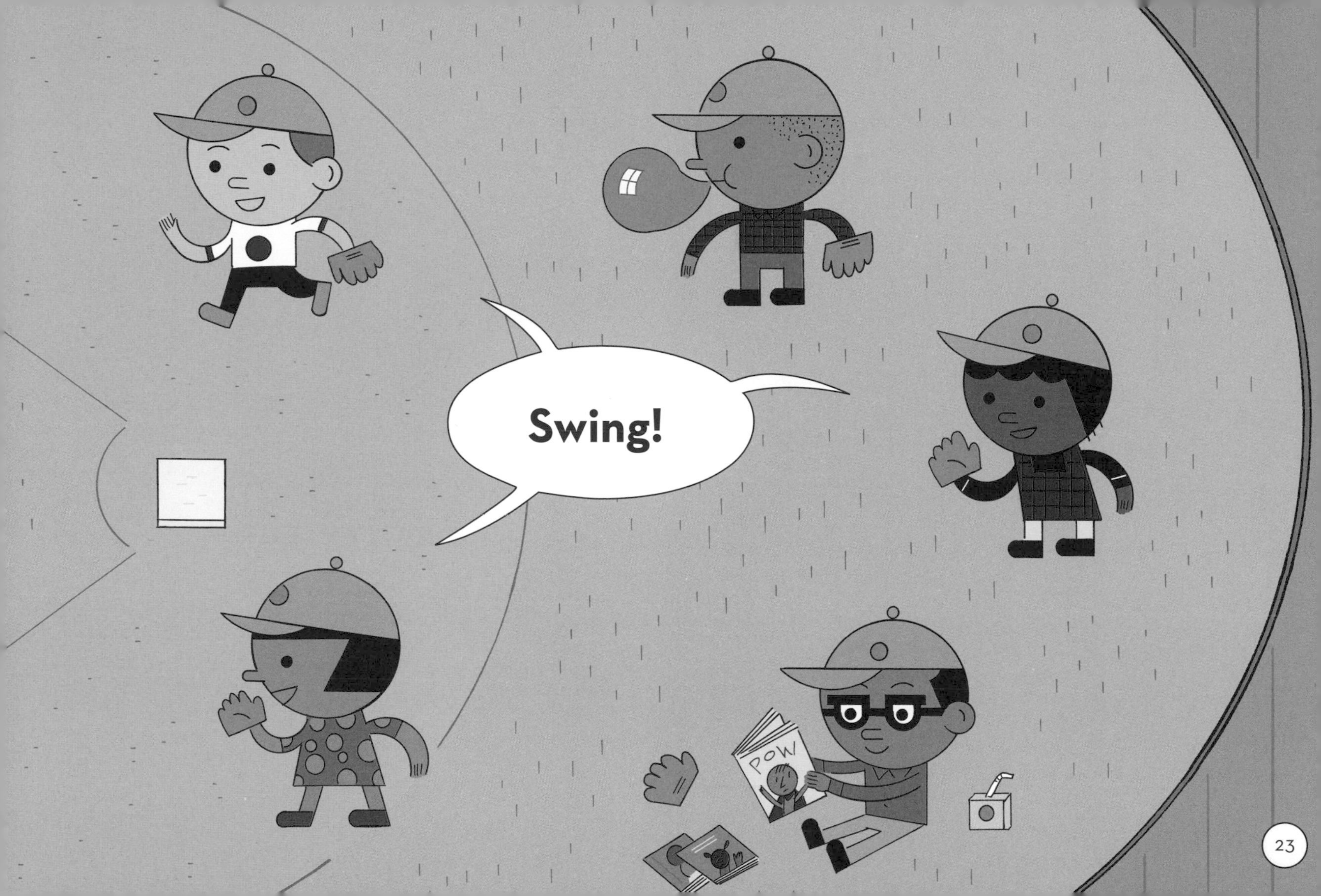
Swing!
POW

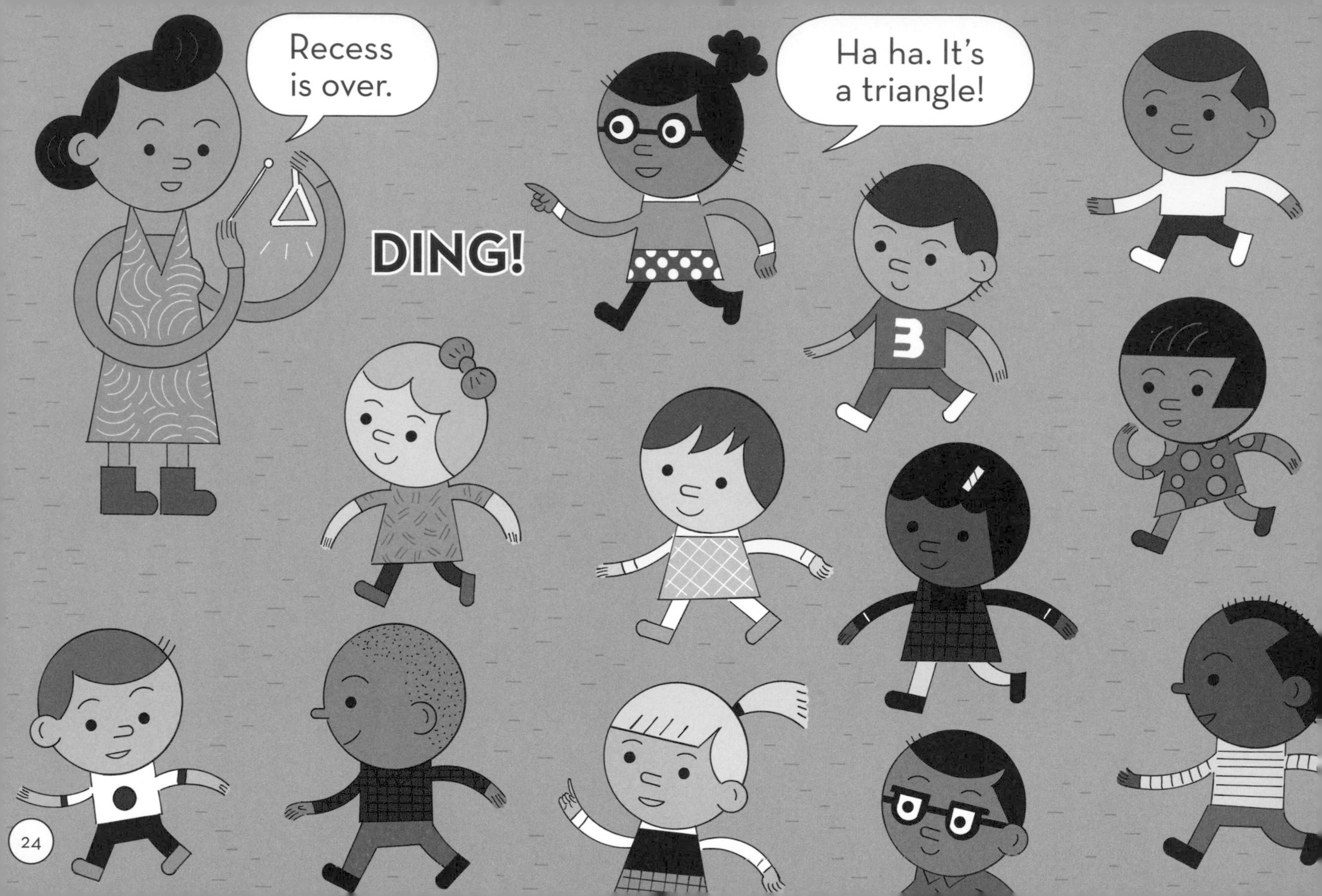
Recess is over.
DING!
Ha ha. It's a triangle!

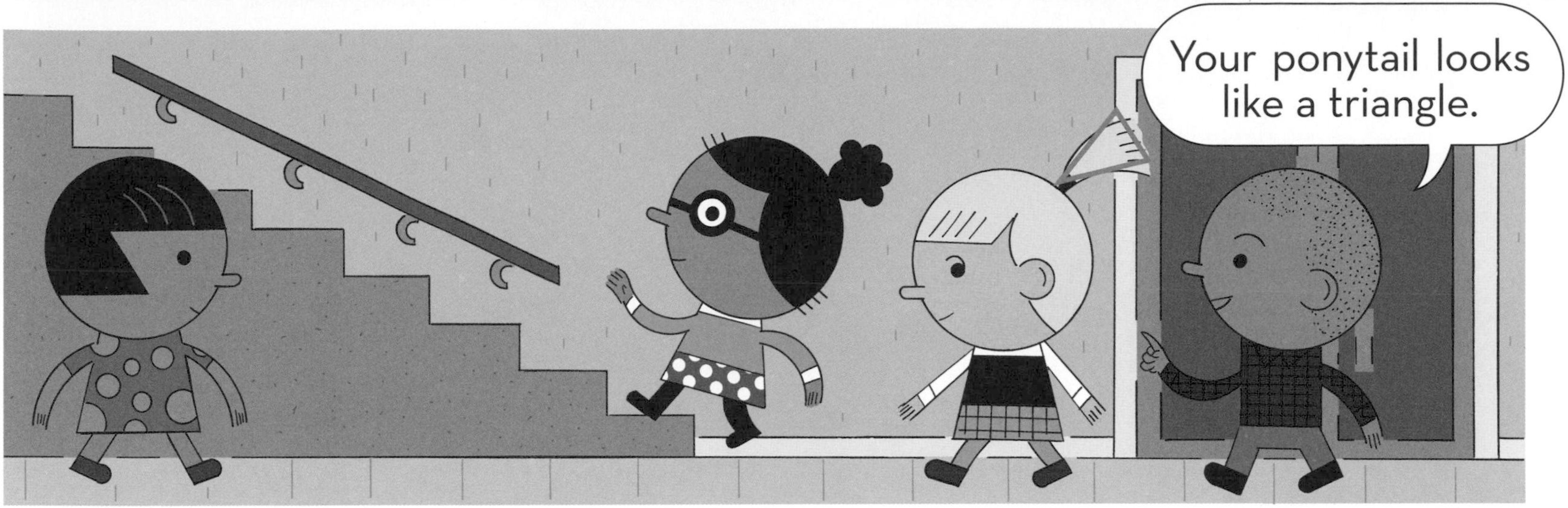
Your ponytail looks like a triangle.

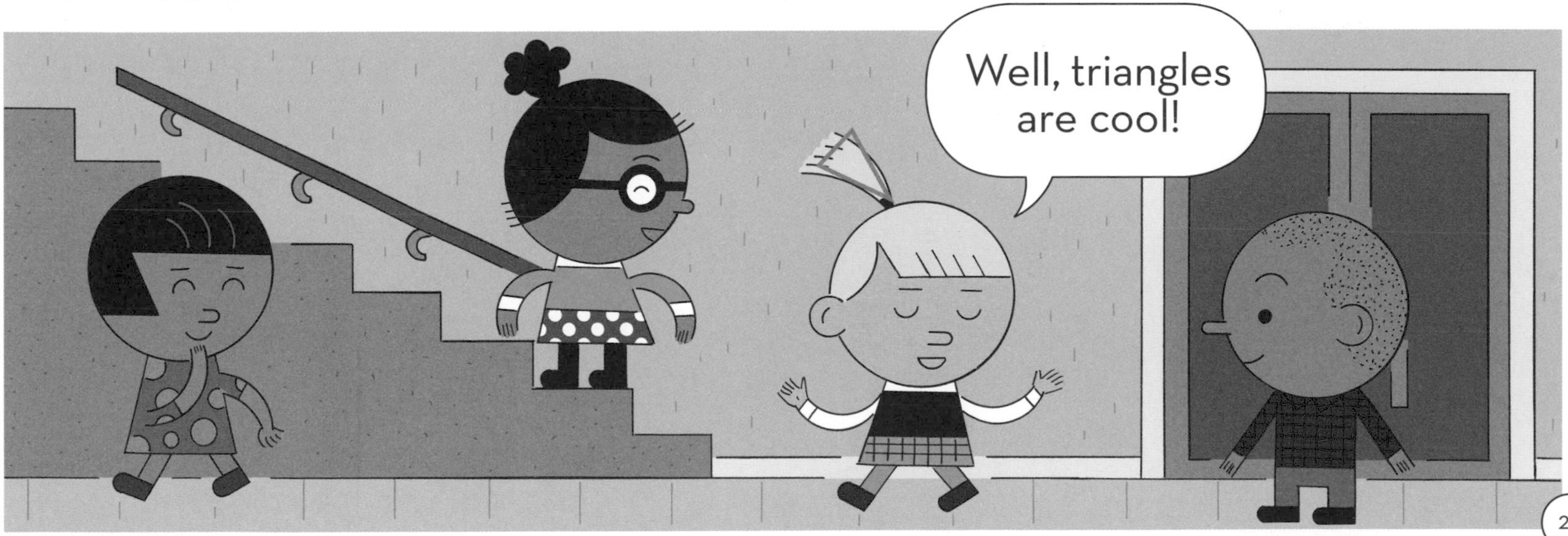
Well, triangles are cool!

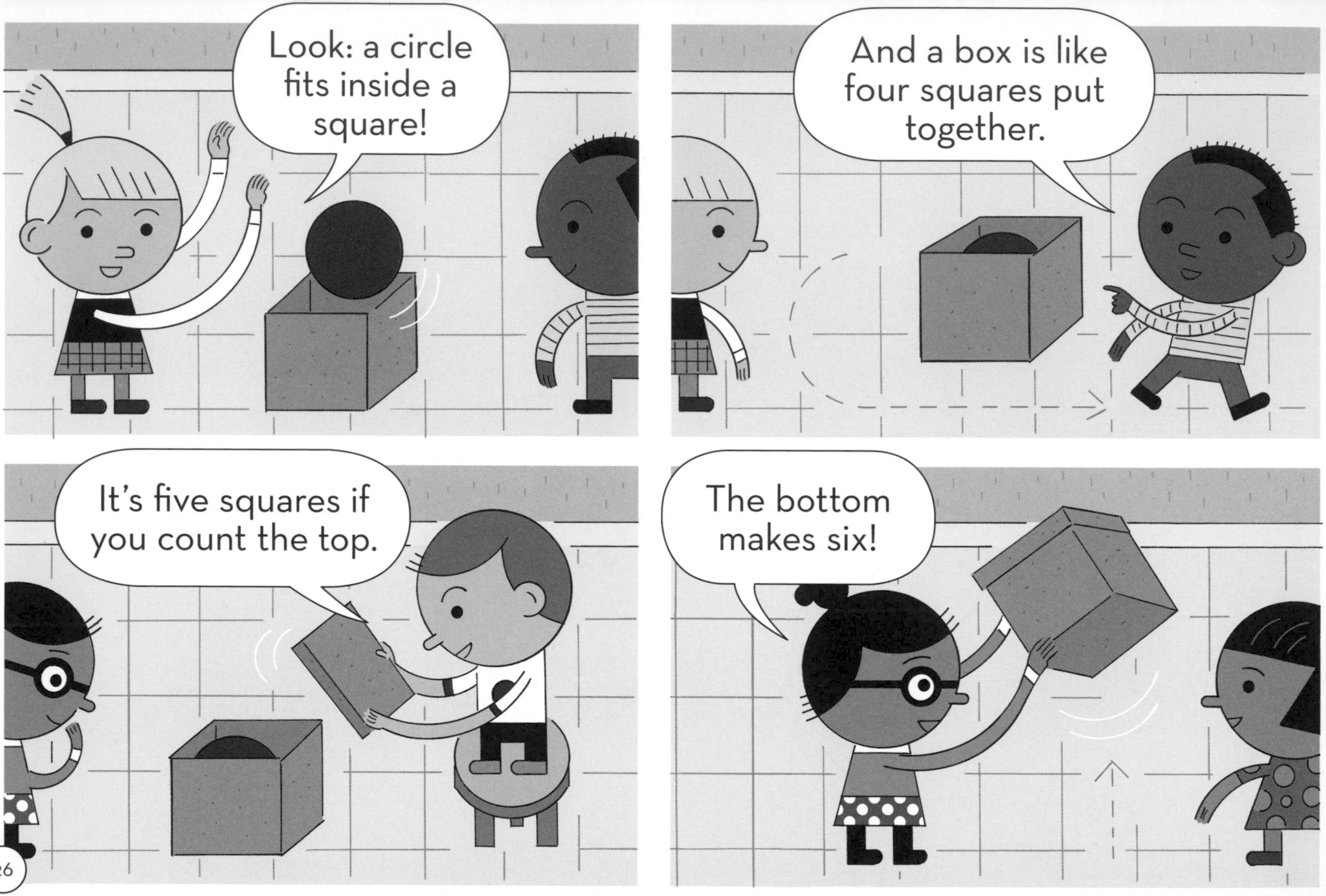
Look: a circle fits inside a square!
And a box is like four squares put together.
It's five squares if you count the top.
The bottom makes six!

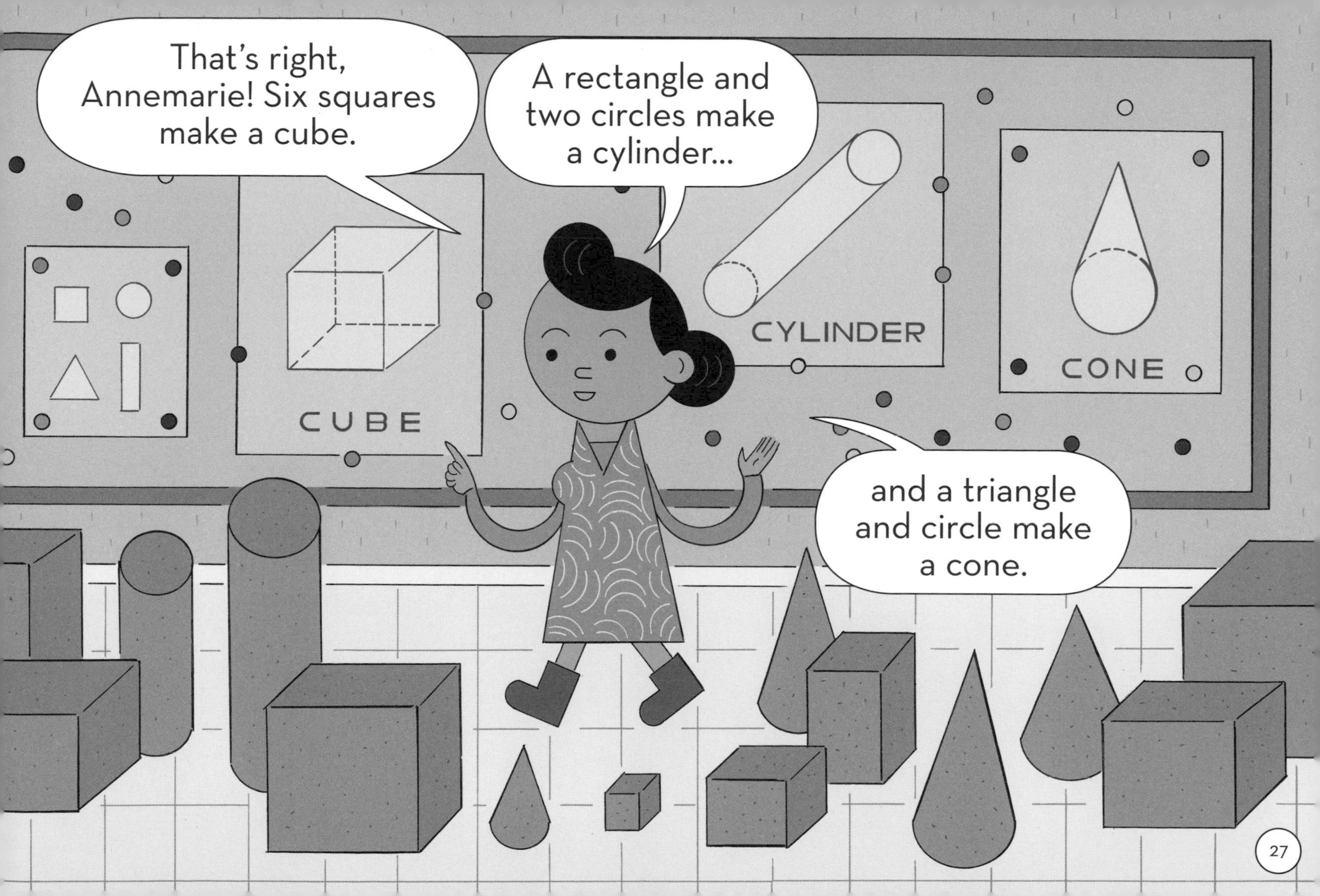
That's right, Annemarie! Six squares make a cube.
A rectangle and two circles make a cylinder...
CUBE
CYLINDER
CONE
and a triangle and circle make a cone.

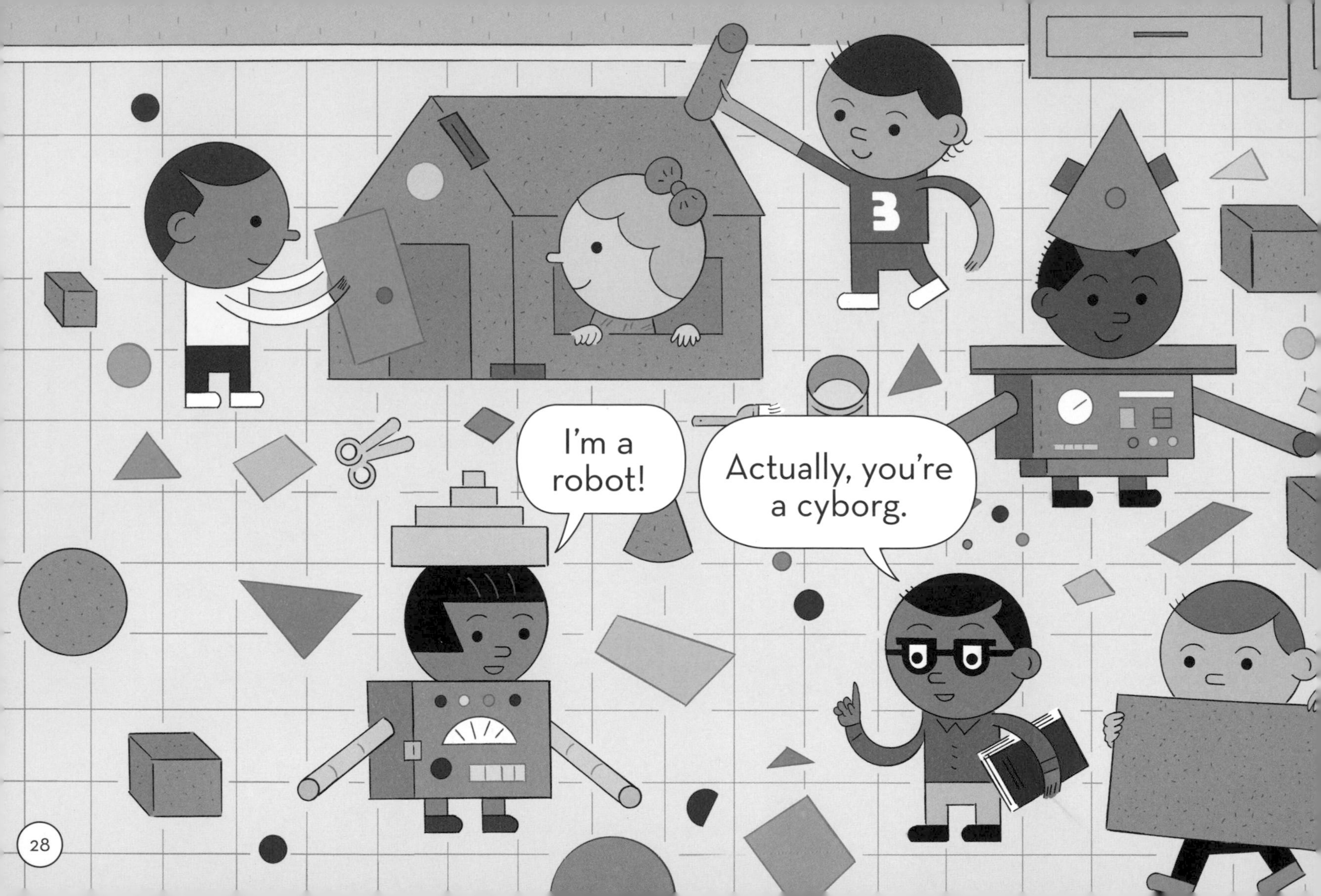
I'm a robot!
Actually, you're a cyborg.

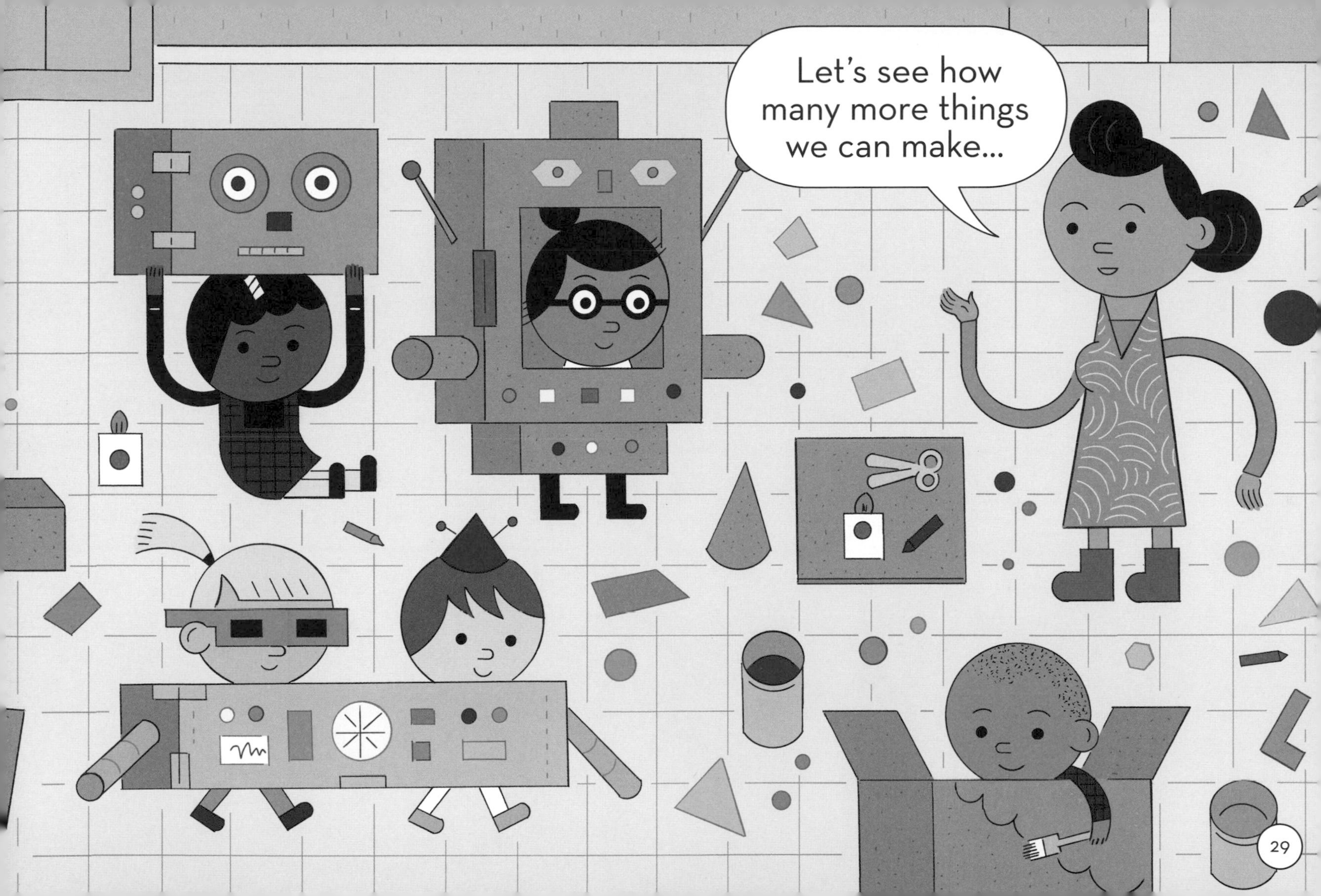
Let’s see how many more things we can make...

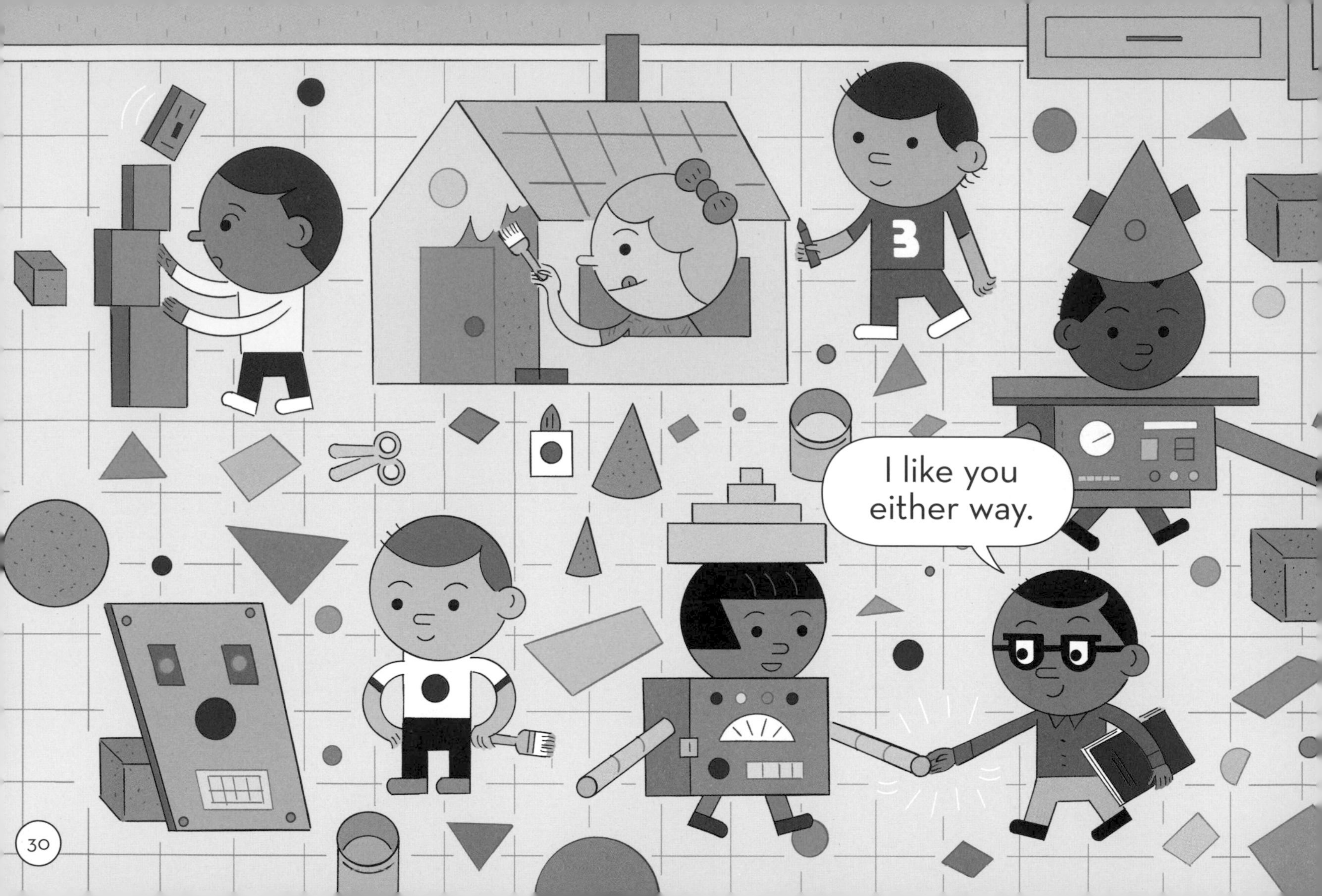
I like you either way.

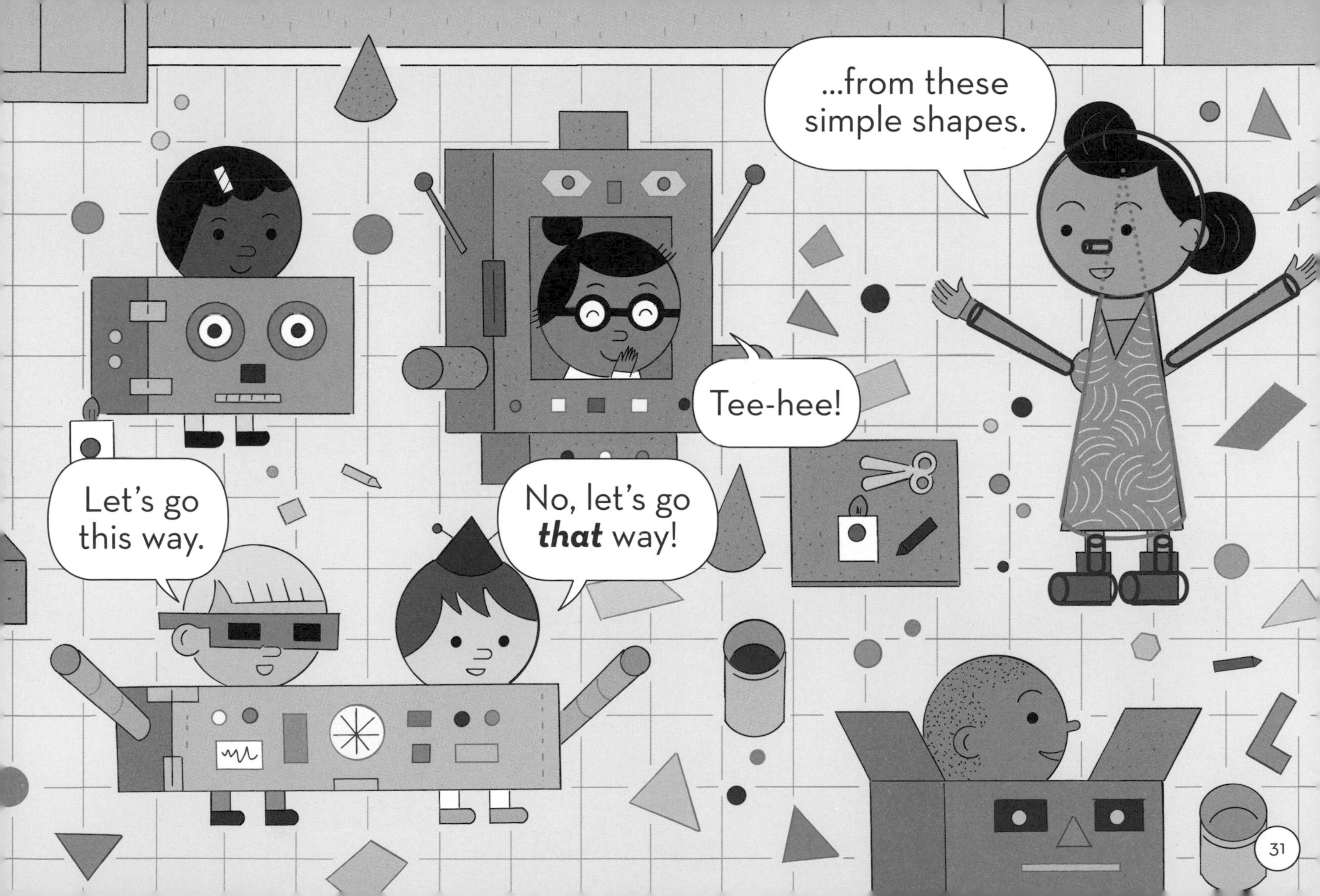
...from these simple shapes.
Tee-hee!
Let's go this way.
No, let's go ***that*** way!

ABOUT THE AUTHOR

As a child, **IVAN BRUNETTI** loved to make images out of simple shapes. Today, he is an art professor as well as an artist and a cartoonist, and he continues to use shapes in his art: "The more you look at this book, the more shapes you'll find. My drawings always start with roughly doodled simple shapes, which I then slowly 'smooth' out. If they start to get too complicated, I try to make them simple again."

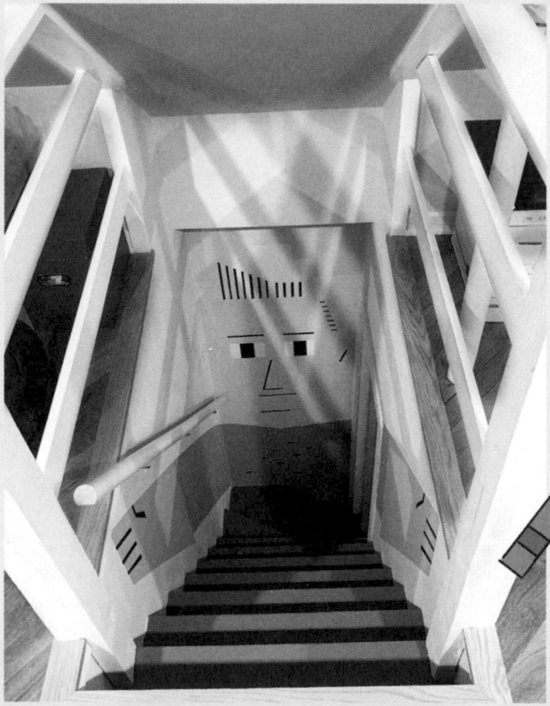

The stairwell in Ivan's studio.

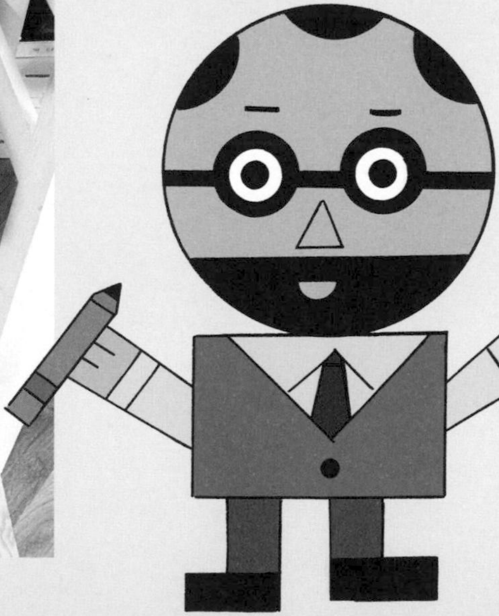

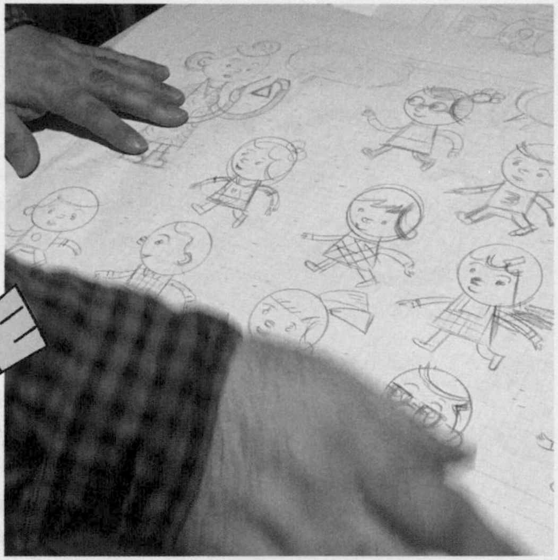

Ivan likes penciling on large sheets of paper.

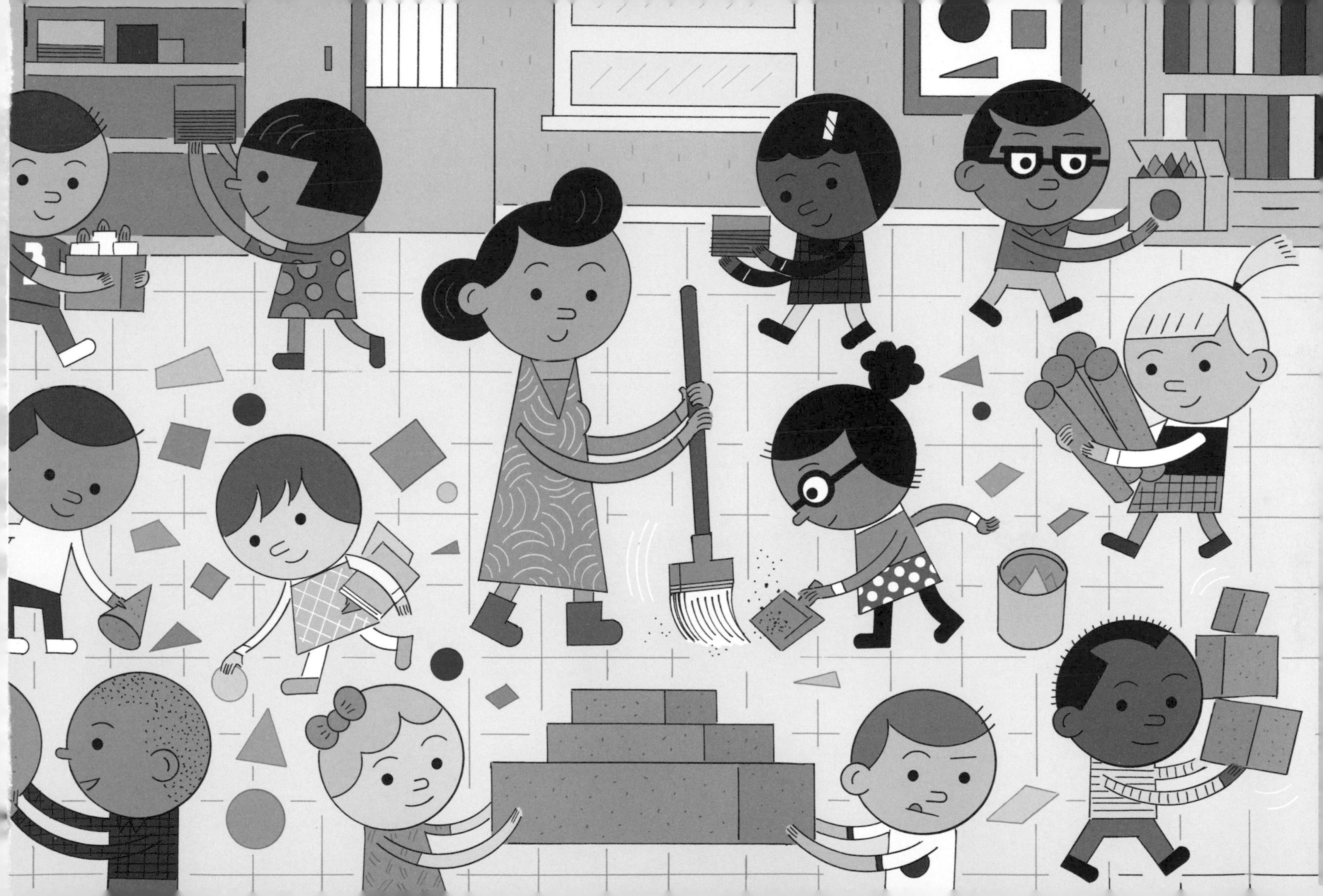

HOW TO READ COMICS WITH KIDS

Kids love comics! They are naturally drawn to the details in the pictures, which make them want to read the words. Comics beg for repeated readings and let both emerging and reluctant readers enjoy complex stories with a rich vocabulary. But since comics have their own grammar, here are a few tips for reading them with kids:

GUIDE YOUNG READERS: Use your finger to show your place in the text, but keep it at the bottom of the character speaking so it doesn't hide the very important facial expressions.

HAM IT UP! Think of the comic book story as a play, and don't hesitate to read with expression and intonation. Assign parts or get kids to supply the sound effects, a great way to reinforce phonics skills.

LET THEM GUESS: Comics provide lots of context for the words, so emerging readers can make informed guesses. Like jigsaw puzzles, comics ask readers to make connections, so check children's understanding by asking, "What's this character thinking?" (But don't be surprised if a kid finds some of the comics' subtle details faster than you.)

TALK ABOUT THE PICTURES: Point out how the artist paces the story with pauses (silent panels) or speeded-up action (a burst of short panels). Discuss how the size and shape of the panels convey meaning.

ABOVE ALL, ENJOY! There is of course never one right way to read, so go for the shared pleasure. Once children make the story happen in their imagination, they have discovered the thrill of reading, and you won't be able to stop them. At that point, just go get them more books—and more comics!

www.TOON-BOOKS.com

SEE OUR FREE ONLINE CARTOON MAKERS, LESSON PLANS, AND MUCH MORE